FAMILIA

FAMILIA

★ *AN AMERICAN STORY OF BETRAYAL AND REVENGE* ★

JOSEPH D. KRINGDON

iUniverse®

FAMILIA
AN AMERICAN STORY OF BETRAYAL AND REVENGE

iUniverse books may be ordered through booksellers or by contacting:

iUniverse
1663 Liberty Drive
Bloomington, IN 47403
www.iuniverse.com
844-349-9409

Because of the dynamic nature of the Internet, any web addresses or links contained in this book may have changed since publication and may no longer be valid. The views expressed in this work are solely those of the author and do not necessarily reflect the views of the publisher, and the publisher hereby disclaims any responsibility for them.

Any people depicted in stock imagery provided by Getty Images are models, and such images are being used for illustrative purposes only. Certain stock imagery © Getty Images.

ISBN: 978-1-6632-1737-0 (sc)
ISBN: 978-1-6632-1738-7 (e)

Library of Congress Control Number: 2021902090

Print information available on the last page.

iUniverse rev. date: 02/03/2021

THE END ... PRESENT DAY

Obituaries. Mom was fascinated by them. She called them the Irish comics, something she had heard from her friends at the office many, many years ago. That always struck me as funny because we're Puerto Rican. She would read each obit and try to piece together the lives of each person, their stories reduced to a few sentences. She often wondered what her own would say. How long would it be? Would they include a picture? Would they mention her passing talents as an artist? Would they talk about her education? Years later when I discovered that most obituaries were paid for by the word, I hid it from her. Unless you were famous or infamous, the words and pictures were not gratis. They were a revenue source for the newspaper, and the content was provided by those who cared enough about you—and were willing to pay for the privilege by the column inch. I could write her obituary, but the confines of both the paper and my budget would not be enough to tell her story.

She was a strong woman who had outgrown a painful childhood. Outspoken without being loud, she was a boss bitch before that term became fashionable. Although only high school educated and up from the streets, she was articulate, studious, and curious. She stood up for herself and anyone she

1

cared about. She had no tolerance for victims or those who felt entitled. She worked and scraped for anything she had, but despite her toughness, she was compassionate and selfless. She didn't need to intimidate others because she commanded respect simply by the way she carried herself. She didn't take any shit. You knew she was in the room. Her presence was felt. Sylvia's name invoked respect.

Now she was dead.

JAMIE

The serene blue sky, white clouds, and seagulls bobbing on the surf outside the window were stark in contrast to the hushed tones and guarded glances inside the room.

Death will do that.

Friends, relatives, associates, and acquaintances bent toward me from time to time. I sat, legs crossed, eyes fixed and received their whispered condolences. A few rubbed my back, while others leaned in to kiss my cheek.

"She looked good ... almost peaceful."

Why is it at every funeral people always feel compelled to tell you how good the lifeless body looks? I wondered. *It's trite. Devoid of original thought.*

I wasn't trying to be a prick. I knew everyone was there to support me and my family. Their presence was offered as a comfort—a show of respect. I just wanted to be left alone. I balled up my fists by my sides in anger. I was a grown-ass fifty-five-year old family man who owned a successful business, but I still did what I did when I was a child. Whenever I was frustrated or angry, I would ball up my fists and hit my head like the two arms of an alarm clock dinging the bell in the middle.

My mother said, "Use your words, *hijo!*" So, there I was, fists rounded, knuckles white, using the words inside my head—the noise so loud I wanted to scream. This wasn't supposed to happen, but it did.

"Jamie, we have to run. Su tio queres ir al casa ahora!"

My mom's best friend from the old neighborhood, Inez—we've always called her aunt—got my attention in Spanglish by telling me that her husband wanted to go home. She called me Jamie, pronounced hi-meh, my given name, although she knew my mother never allowed that. She wanted me to be American.

"Hijo, don't let people call you Jamie. Introduce yourself, and insist on being called James, not Jim or Jimmie! You are American-born ... with class. *Entiendes?*"

Inez knew this but always found a way to remind us that we were the same: Latino, from the neighborhood. I'd like to think she was being kind. Truth be told, my given name was taken from me a long time ago back in the neighborhood. I was a stocky child and my mom shopped for me in the husky section of the department store. I was tagged Gordo, the opposite of slim, forever more by my friends, and despite my mother's protestations, my siblings called me Jamie.

Holding my face squarely, Inez hugged me tightly, looked me in the eyes, and offered an anguished smile. She seemed to be searching for words. It clearly pained her too much. She and my mom had known each other all their lives. They had schemed as teenagers and planned as adults, still squeezing each other's hands and giggling conspiratorially. They didn't need words. They had history. They had each other.

I grabbed Inez's hands and pulled her closer to me, enveloping this small woman with my body. For just a moment, I thought I could stop the loneliness my mother's passing seemed to bring.

I sobbed softly. Inez smelled like my mother. She broke the embrace, tears in her eyes, and let her hand pass over my cheek.

"Lo siento! Que Dios te bendiga," she said. That's when the drumbeat of my heart started again.

GORDO

Too tired to take off the clothes from today's funeral, I sat quietly in my office. I was upstairs from where today's festivities—if you could call them that—took place. Pictures stared down from the walls above me—images in black and white that spanned decades, each of a different occasion, a different emotion ... a different me. Somehow I felt my presence in the room tainted the innocence these pictures captured. I slumped over my desk. I took a deep breath. My heart sounded like a conga drum. My entire being was in conflict with the memories that hung from the walls.

There was the Little League picture of a ragtag group of players, Eddy Cepeda, Rappy, Willy Cullen, and me, all smiling at the camera, uniforms ill-fitting, caps askew, but happy. We had just won the church league championship. We played at Colgate Field, a browned-out diamond just off the busy Bruckner Expressway in the South Bronx. Willy was our catcher, and the equipment barely covered his blocklike frame. His life at home was so messed up that he took to dressing in his uniform and catcher's equipment the night before a game and shlepping out to the field to camp out on home plate where he waited for us to wake him when we arrived to play the next day.

Rappy was our overactive shortstop, and his chatter, muted in this picture, was more legendary than his batting average. Eddy, our star, had dirt all over his uniform as evidence of his on-field hustle and desire. And me, the youngest by a few years, was the pitcher who threw straight and hard, my Yankee warm-up jacket covering the top of my jersey.

I looked at the gun on my desk, then to the cigar smoldering in the ashtray, and then up again at the picture gallery. The conga was louder inside my ears. I heard my breathing, the long draw in and the hard exhale. My chin felt heavy in my hands. My eye caught the picture of a small boy with a crew cut dressed in a polo shirt and dungarees, his arms around his gang. Again, I was the youngest of the group, which included Eddy, Rappy, and Willy. The collage of photos documented my evolution— my family's evolution. It was a mosaic that amplified both the joy and pain that served as the soundtrack to our lives.

"What do you know? What did you know?" I whispered.

I began to reach for the gun but stuttered. I stared down at my desk, shook my head clean, and grabbed the cigar instead. I took a long pull with my eyes closed, found the gun with my empty hand, and felt the conga in my ears.

Is this how the Japanese commit suicide? Is this how Roman soldiers throw themselves upon their swords? I wondered. A gun in the mouth seemed cowardly in comparison. Maybe the passage of time eroded the horror, the blood, the mess, the pity, and the desperation left behind for others to clean up. Perhaps time canonized the act into heroics and daring. Perhaps the years lionized the defeat and cowardice like the death of Yeats or Romeo.

I couldn't even shoot myself without a fucking intellectual internal dialogue. I'd do better to cut out my tongue before shooting myself in the mouth. The bloody tongue on my desk

7

would suffice enough as a final note. Better yet, I could just cut out my tongue and suffer forever. It would serve as a reminder to my transgression—my fucking scarlet letter. God bless fucking America. Why couldn't I just do this?! I blew out a deep breath through my nose and dropped both the gun and the cigar. I clenched my fists by my sides, balled them up, and started to bang my head on either side for just a moment. For a minute, I was a twelve-year-boy. Afterward, I inserted my right fist in my mouth and screamed.

Flashbulbs in my mind were like the paparazzi catching someone coming out of a club. The staccato of the flashes was a strobe light pulsing inside my head. I pointed the gun at the photographs and wondered what I was thinking at the moment each picture was taken.

I was tired. I rested my head sideways on my gun. The metal was cold. I drew deeply on my cigar, closed my eyes, held the breath, and eased it out.

I swallowed the barrel of the gun.

"Half is done when the work is begun!" I blurted out mindlessly.

This was a phrase from one of my kid's old videos. I heard the terrible, stilted imitation of a British accent from a grown man dressed up as a bird.

"Half is done when the work is begun!"

Hahf... The Brahmin pronunciation somehow made sense. *Strange how the little voice chimes in just now. Maybe it's Lucifer calling.* "*Hahf* is done when the work is begun!"

The metal was cold in my mouth. In a few seconds, it warmed, and I closed my eyes. I saw my black-and-white self in the photos, my mother lying in a pool of blood on the street.

THE PACKAGE

It was addressed to me with my mom's name and return address as the sender. The postal cancellation was from her local post office. Inside, I found a small bottle of hot sauce along with a note that read:

"Like brother, like son ..."

It didn't make sense. When I called her to inquire about the package, I could tell she was confused at first. Maybe she was slipping in her old age. When I described its contents, I thought I heard her draw her breath sharply, as though whatever I just told her took it away deeply and suddenly. But she gathered herself.

"Mijo, I'm sorry, I meant to send that to someone else. I guess I had you on my mind when I was writing the address. I'll come and get it from you right now."

My mother never made mindless mistakes like that, and she never rushed to my house for anything. She knew I would stop by her home sometime during the week, and whatever she needed from me could usually wait until then. It was odd that she would react as she did. When we hung up from our conversation, I stared at the note and then the bottle, shook my head, and moved on with my day. Yet, there was something about my mother's reaction that stayed behind like the lyrics to a song I was familiar with but couldn't identify.

Suddenly, a thought occurred to me: *The hot sauce! It is not one of the usual brands. It is extra picante (spicy), and it was the last thing placed in my uncle Jackie's—my mother's brother's—casket at his funeral many years ago by someone who always scared the shit out of me.*

EDDY

Eduardo "Eddy" Cepeda was a lifelong FBI guy. He grew up in my neighborhood in the South Bronx. Eddy was perpetually ready for any street game—stickball, stoopball, curbball, fire-escape basketball, or Johnny on the pony—and he was good at all of them. He moved naturally, gliding along the cracked sidewalks and stones, faster and more effortlessly than the rest of us.

Oh, he was smart! Street-smart and book smart. A voracious reader, he skipped the second grade. His teachers encouraged him to apply to the prestigious Bronx High School of Science, but his combination of intelligence and athletics made him a natural for Dewitt Clinton, where he became a ferocious defensive back and a merit scholar. All-city and all-state, he accepted an athletic scholarship to Holy Cross. During Eddy's senior year, the Crusaders would be the last to beat mighty Boston College in their annual square off. Eddy intercepted a Boston College pass and ran it back eighty yards. The press called it a crucial turning point in the game. Wall Street and Fortune 500 firms came calling, but Eddy always wanted to be an FBI agent.

With his Latin heritage and his facility for both English and Spanish, Eddy served the FBI in Miami and Texas. He easily fit in among the hustlers and gang members who worked in the shadows of southern Florida and Tex-Mex border towns. He had been a street kid—a chameleon in these surroundings. His assumed identities were a composite partially of all the characters he grew up with. Eddy's fluidity allowed him to move freely and gain the confidence of virtually anyone he encountered.

Several decades in the field earned him his fair share of scar tissue, both mentally and physically. Finally, when his close calls started to outdistance his conviction rate, he knew it was time to pull the pin on his career. He bought a condo on the shores of Isla Verde, just outside of San Juan. His kids were grown and on their own. His wife had died in a car accident a few years into his toughest assignment, and he never thought it fit or fair to invite another into his crazy life.

It was to this condo that I mailed a small, nondescript package with a note and a phone, no return address.

Eddy woke very early most mornings without an alarm. Once awake, he put on the workout clothes he had carefully laid out the night before. He grabbed his iPhone, his earbuds, and his dog and headed out the door for a run along the beach. It was twenty-one steps down three sets of stairs to the back of his condo and onto the sand. Eddy counted everything. He said it was for planning purposes, but it was really for the sense of control and calm it provided. Once on the beach, he ran from one end to the other, ticking off goals—the lifeguard chair, the outdoor hotel bar, the pool, and the people walking the beach at this early hour. Passing each was like the collecting of small tokens by a video game character who was jumping, hopping, or running along the sand. Eddy saw everything while he ran and somehow still kept score. Coal, Eddy's German shepherd-black lab mutt, dutifully and enthusiastically kept pace, wagging his tail and moving his head side to side as though sweeping the area for unfriendlies. Coal met Eddy's stride; languid or determined, he matched every change in gait. Eddy was determined this morning, feet pounding the sand, body leaning forward, and arms pumping like pistons. His body bounded forward with energy, while his mind raced. Listening to B-Tribe with their distinct Latin beat, flamenco guitar textures and haunting club sound, his thoughts danced with questions. A package arrived yesterday with a note telling him to use the enclosed phone to call a number at eleven o'clock this morning. The package smelled slightly of cigar smoke but would be free of fingerprints, its path obscured and circuitous. The message was neatly handwritten, almost like a Catholic school-kid copying a penmanship assignment. It was signed "Gordo Flaco."

Gordo Flaco was a phrase that only one person he knew would invoke—someone who had history with Eddy and whom he cared for dearly. So he knew he would follow the note's directions, but he spent most of last night and today's run wondering why the tradecraft for a conversation between lifelong friends.

FLACO AND GORDO

Eddy was a little like a slightly older big brother. While each weekday was filled with school and family activities, every Saturday was like the opening day of the Olympics on my block. Dragged from bed most school mornings to bathe, drink hot chocolate, and eat a piece of toast in front of an open stove for warmth before hitting the pavement for the walk to PS 48, I was less than enthusiastic to start the day. Conversely, on Saturday mornings, I was up as the sun came up. Jumping into my dungarees, polo shirt and Chuck Taylor sneakers, I raced outside to make sure I was among the first to organize or get picked for many punchball, stoopball, fire-escape basketball, or curbball games that were to come during the day.

Cleary, as one the best athletes—he was sleek Flaco, the opposite of fat—Eddy was almost always a captain. He sized up his options, and while I was a roly-poly kid—nicknamed Gordo—I had great eye-hand coordination. As a later round selection when teams were chosen, I represented real value with my hustle and a practiced game. He would tease me by seeming to contemplate choosing me or another kid, with his eye movement from one of us to the other, but he always eventually chose me ... unless someone beat him to it. Eddy taught me teamwork, hustle, and finesse. He modeled how to play hard to win without cheating or being a sore loser. He also taught me to dance and how to rap to a girl, but that was later. Eddy left for college, but we never lost touch. He set a path for me to follow: study hard, win a scholarship, and move beyond the neighborhood.

I had questions about my mother's death during a so-called robbery, and Eddy was the only one who wouldn't doubt them.

By eleven o'clock in the morning, I had driven thirty miles in one direction and then thirty miles in another direction, crossing over two state lines, just to be sure no one was following. Finally, I pulled into a rest stop and took out the burner to wait for Eddy's call. My phone started buzzing right at the appointed hour.

"Flaco, comò esta mi amigo?" I said.

"Bien, Gordo, que tal? (What's up?) Porque la capa y la daga? (Why the cloak and dagger?)"

"Eddy, I know you came to my mom's services and we only had a quick conversation about her death, but I think it's all bogus."

"Bogus?"

"Yes, she was shot at close range, center mass, two shots after *supposedly* struggling to keep her iPhone away from two dudes who rolled up on her on a motorcycle."

"Gordo, I had heard there were a rash of these bandito robberies in that neighborhood from these kids on bikes grabbing smartphones, no?"

"True, but they started up only about three months ago."

I hesitated for a second before continuing.

"Maybe I'm imagining this, but my mom started getting nostalgic for the old neighborhood around the same time and was making weekly trips to the old market to pick up pernil y espeicas. It doesn't make sense. You know after we managed to move north, she never wanted to go back down there—ever."

"So?" Eddy questioned.

"Eddy, my mom had not been back to the old neighborhood in decades. She cut off all contact with people down there when she moved us all up north to Connecticut. I think she was avoiding something or someone. She was always nervous about running into someone she might have known from the old days. Her excuse was always that we had moved on. There was nothing for us back there. Then all of a sudden she starts sneaking down there for food?"

"So?"

"Maybe it's not connected, but—"

"But what?"

"I got a package from my mom, or so it seemed. It was a bottle of hot sauce with a very strange note."

"Hot sauce? Strange note?"

"Yeah, the hot sauce was a very specific brand, muy picante, that my uncle loved," I explained and continued.

"In fact, he was the only one I ever saw that used this kind. I think he got it at a specialty store in the city or maybe someone had it shipped in for him"

"I'm not getting it."

"The note said, 'like brother, like son.'"

"So?"

"Well, when my uncle, her brother, died— *in an accident*— someone placed a bottle of this brand of hot sauce in his casket as a going away gesture. Someone who always spooked me. I don't think my mom sent me that box. I think someone made it seem like my mom sent it to me, knowing I'd call my mom and ask her about it. When I did ask her about it, she seemed quietly shocked and then told me she made a mistake and meant to send it to someone else."

"Did you question her?"

"It didn't seem important, but I should have. It's my fault she's dead. I can't shake that feeling ..." I choke up and couldn't complete my sentence.

"It's not your fault!"

I could feel my fists ball up at my sides.

"But it is ... I should've ..." I broke off my thought and cried softly.

Eddy didn't say anything, knowing that there was not much he could do to assuage my feeling of guilt over actions not taken, at least not now.

Gathering myself, I said, "Eddy, I'm sorry. This has been all too overwhelming for me"

"It's OK."

"I realize now that my mom started taking her trips back to the old hood shortly after I told her about the package."

"I still don't see the connection."

"I think the package was a message or a summons meant for my mom that I unknowingly delivered to her. And it sent her to her death," I said.

"Tell me about these trips."

"First, when she went down there, she always insisted on going alone. *Siempre!* Second, you know my mom. She's fairly casual in her dress. When she was heading down to the old neighborhood, she dressed all Jackie Onassis—dark sunglasses, dark scarf over her head, and gloves."

"You think she was seeing someone?" Eddy asked.

"It was more like she was trying to avoid seeing someone or going incognito, like a celeb, you know, trying to move around in their everyday life so no one recognizes them."

"Avoiding detection or identification?"

"That's just it, Eddy; I don't know. The other thing that bothers me is that the two guys on motorcycles wore dark helmets, dark visors, leather jackets, and gloves like they didn't want to be detected or identified either. A few of the witnesses said my mother *didn't* struggle when they grabbed her iPhone, yet one of the dudes screamed something very loudly and fired the shots."

"What did he scream?"

"No one is sure. It was so loud it scared the shit out of the onlookers, but the iPhone was found on the street a few blocks away."

"Like it wasn't the real objective of the robbery?"

"Exactly! I think whoever set this up—and I know it sounds crazy—used the package that was sent to me as a message to my mother."

"You mentioned that someone—someone who scared you—placed that same brand of hot sauce in your uncle's casket. Who was that?"

I did not answer right away. Instead, I contemplated the consequences of the answer and the ugly road it might take us down.

Finally, I answered.

"It was Tomas Montenegro."

"Oh, shit! Wasn't his sister married to your uncle?"

"Yeah, but as you know, he's also Un Jefe—a big boss—in the Doble Doble."

Eddy was quiet for a second. He was sure the local police chalked up Sylvia's death to a robbery gone bad. The previous crimes with the same MO in the area would sway their thinking. If he were investigating, Eddy would have questions. Were the previous banditos outfitted in the same mysterious

18

way? Was it the same bikes and the same banditos? Did the other events invoke violence? Did this rash of robberies die down after the shooting? These small facts meant nothing apart from one another, but together, they might reveal things. But Eddy understood that in the hood, crime and violence were so common they numbed any sense of curiosity from law enforcement. It was much easier and more expedient to assume the obvious—less paperwork or overtime. This seemed to be a classic case of confirmation bias where the preconceived notion is hardly challenged.

"G, What are you saying, man? You think someone like the Doble Doble set up and offed your moms on purpose?"

"Yes!"

"But why?"

"I don't know."

"And you want me to look into it, si?"

"Please."

Eddy thought for a quick second.

"I've got to make some calls."

"Thank you. Really," I told him.

"I'll be on the first flight to New York. I'll be in touch. Keep that burner close. Hasta mañana!"

MONTENEGRO DOBLE DOBLE

The Montenegro Doble Doble was a crime family that came up in Spanish Harlem. The Montenegros had two sets of twin brothers—thus, the double double—born in the early 1930s sandwiched between daughters. The two sets of twins were born twenty months apart. They roamed the streets in a pack as teenagers. Paolo and Pedro comprised the first set of twins, while Tomas and Timoteo were the second set. They rustled all the local kids and hustled any stranger who dared to come into their neighborhood. Like most career criminals, they started out with no long-range plans, just short schemes and petty crimes to get them what they needed now. Smarter than most and disarming in their appearance—dark eyes set against skin more white than brown and jet-black hair—they charmed most of their quarry. If that didn't prove effective, they enjoyed employing brute force for persuasion. As their crimes increased, their reputations and ambition grew to legendary proportions. Their perceived success—clothing, cars, and jewelry—attracted willing lieutenants and motivated muscle. They moved easily from muggings to gambling, protection schemes, robberies, prostitution, and, eventually, into the drug trade.

Their little street gang had grown into a far-reaching syndicate that had branches throughout the boroughs and in other pockets of poor Latino communities throughout the country from Florida to Texas and beyond to California. Their hustles had matured into a business that was fully integrated and diversified with many levels of management and workers, as well as products and services. They had competitors to either appease and collaborate with or battle and eliminate. They had grown up hard and demanded fidelity. They paid their acolytes often and well enough to keep them in line and loyal. The Doble Doble managed their stable well. On occasion, an employee who did not understand the rules of engagement was dismissed publicly and *permanently*.

The Montenegros were atypical benevolent overseers and ruthless enforcers. Anyone who lived on their turf knew the rules. Eddy was very familiar with them, not only from growing up in the neighborhood but from their repeated brushes with the law. While his past assignments put him in some proximity to their operations, he was never allowed to work directly on their cases. He was too well known to them. Instead, he was used as a shadow advisor—someone who was consulted around strategy and approaches to the Doble Doble. It was too dangerous for him to be directly involved. The bureau wanted to avoid any potential conflicts of interest the Doble Doble could potentially exploit.

Paolo and Pedro were the suave and charismatic leaders. They engendered the confidence and loyalty of their armies. Tomas was the brains of the outfit. Like a savvy military leader, he had the ability to anticipate the maneuvers of both his allies and his enemies before they even contemplated these steps themselves. It was said that Tomas could see around corners and deal with problems before they occurred. He was the most patient and methodical while excelling at mapping out long-range plans. He also meted out praise or punishment as required. Tomas admired and studied military history as a guidepost to his moves and saw himself as a field general. He was the most feared of the brothers, deliberate and decisive in his actions. Timoteo was the most laid back. Not to suggest that he didn't share his brother's talents for intimidation and persuasion, but his charms were of the understated variety.

RAPPY

Rafael Arroyo was what was once called an overactive kid. This excess energy had him flitting from here to there through the neighborhood. In school, he was always talking, always moving, and always getting in trouble. On the streets, he was constantly in everyone's business, worried he was missing something. He was slightly annoying but harmless. Kids started likening him to a fly because he buzzed. Most of us tolerated him, knowing he'd move on quickly. His family called him Raffi, but his father, who owned the local mercado said that his son moved around *muy rapido*, and took to calling him Rapido. Eventually, this was shortened to a nickname that hewed closer to his own: Rappy. It stuck.

Rappy worked at his father's mercado, Leche y Cosas, most days. It was the daily social center of the neighborhood. People moved in and out to buy newspapers, milk, cheese, coffee, cigarettes, and sandwiches and to catch up on the latest happenings or gossip. It was open from six o'clock in the morning until ten o'clock at night seven days a week. It was a busy place. Aside from stocking the necessities, the mercado also sold the original dollar and a dream before the legal lottery with the numbers game. Local patrons would go to the back of the store and pay a dollar to select three digits that they hoped would match the randomly drawn last three numbers of the local handle calculated at the racetrack that day and published in the newspaper the next. Rappy would take the bets and write down the numbers selected in his book and give a receipt of the same to each player. His father always double-checked Rappy's work; surprisingly, he never found it wanting. Rappy handled the intake and the payouts. Of course, this racket was completely illegal and off the books. The mercado was a branch office for a larger criminal operation run by the local Montenegros. Rappy moved up from order taker to bag man, eventually running all the moving parts of their branch before leaving for college.

He attended the University of Miami because he liked the weather—and the women—in southern Florida. He studied business and, owing to his prior work, concentrated his studies in statistics. While he was an average student in most of his other studies, his work with numbers was impressive enough to earn him a recommendation from one of his professors for an internship at a local logistics company in Miami. Rappy graduated with a job offer at this company and over the years worked his way up to being a partner at the firm. Eventually, he bought out the majority of his aging partners and renamed the company Rapido Mundo—A Global Logistics Company.

Rappy worked with truckers, shippers, conglomerates, and local businesses, helping them navigate and plan the movement of goods and services along an interconnected global supply chain from their point of origin to their eventual consumption. Given the nature of his work and his location's proximity to Latin America, he had various government agencies auditing his books and tracing his work orders in an effort to discover illegal traffickers. With Rappy's family's prior association with Doble Doble, there were always rumors about his true clients and/or his silent partners. Whatever the association, it could not be proven in a court of law.

Eddy had heard the rumors. Despite this, he kept in touch with Rappy over the years. Careful not to mix his business with his friendship, his conversations were always lighthearted.

Rappy's father still owned the mercado, and Eddy found it useful from time to time to fact-check stories and rumors in the old neighborhood. Rappy was not only at the nexus of all the information at the mercado but loved the back-and-forth required to tease out all the juicy details. He still immersed himself in the minutiae during his weekly phone calls with his parents. He couldn't help himself. He needed to be in the know. In his business, information was currency.

Eddy needed information. With every investigation, he needed to gather pieces from various sources. When laid out, these tidbits would start to form a mosaic. At first, disparate, but eventually, a thesis formed. Eddy dialed Rappy at his office.

"Rapido Mundo, this is Rappy. How can I help you?"

"Hermano, it's Eddy."

"Yo, man, did you change cells? Your name didn't come up on the caller ID."

"Oh, sorry. Old habits."

"If you change numbers, how do people know how to get in touch with you?" Rappy asked.

"They don't," Eddy admitted. "I forward the old number to my new number and then only answer the calls I recognize."

"What about texts to the old number?"

"Same procedure. I keep the old phone for a bit and only answer those people I recognize."

"OK, I get it. What's going on, brother? Need some info from the old neighborhood?"

"Well, sort of," Eddy began. "You know Gordo's mom died in robbery gone bad, right?"

The question was met with a pause. Eddy's spidey sense started to tingle.

"Yeah, I heard that. Sorry I couldn't get back for the services. She wasn't tight with anyone after they left the neighborhood, though. I mean, they practically disappeared."

"You hear anything about the accident?"

"Not much, man. I heard that there were a few of those motorcycle bandits roaming the streets taking people for their smartphones. Happened a couple of times if I'm not mistaken. She was the latest and took a bullet after refusing to let go of her device."

"That's just it. Witnesses say she gave up her phone willingly but was shot anyway. Other victims, even the ones who wouldn't give up the phone, weren't touched."

"What are you saying?" Rappy questioned.

"I'm not sure. Just don't like the fact pattern," Eddy parried.

"What's it to you? I thought you were retired."

Eddy ignored Rappy's question and carefully thought about his next question.

"Rappy, you hear anything about the Doble Doble in this?"

There was silence. The pregnant kind.

Rappy feigned an interruption.

"Eddy, can you hold on a second ..."

Rappy put Eddy on hold. He closed the door to his office, removed one of the many burner phones he kept in his office drawer, studied Eddy's mobile number on his office phone, and then immediately texted Eddy in all caps:

"EDDY, NOT HERE ... NOT ON THIS CALL ... NOT ABOUT DD"

Eddy heard the ping of his texts and glanced at it quickly.

Rappy got back on the line.

"Hey, Eddy," he said. "I got a fire I have to put out here. OK if we talk some other time?"

Rappy texted Eddy again:

"CALL ME TONIGHT ON THIS PHONE."

"Sure. No problem," Eddy replied.

"Thanks, Eddy. Got to go!"

That evening Eddy called Rappy's burner.

Rappy explained to Eddy that he never knew who was listening on his phones. He could not afford to have any talk of the Doble Doble associated with Rapido Mundo. He said he didn't know much but had heard some things in the last few months.

"Like what?" Eddy questioned.

Rappy was hesitant at first. With a little coaxing from Eddy, Rappy unwound quite a tale.

The story went that back in the day, someone dropped a dime on the Doble Doble in the Bronx. A source conspired with the Feds to ensnare the Montenegro twins in enough illegal activities to put them away for a while. Eddy remembered that the cases were brought before the courts, but the evidence was only strong enough to convict three of the four brothers. The cases were solid against Paolo and Pedro (the oldest twins) as well as Tomas, while there was only circumstantial evidence, loosely assembled, against Timoteo. Using the weakness of the case against Timoteo, the three brothers bargained their time for his freedom. Eddy's recollection of these events synched up with Rappy's retelling, and this is where the story turned twisted.

Timoteo was the youngest of the boys by mere minutes, but he was always the most diminutive. It was only a matter of degrees, but he was more the lover of the group, not the fighter the other three were. While they were ruthless, he was merely mean. His brothers' presence offered him protection. There was a sense, cultivated from their upbringing, that the twins traveled in packs. Timoteo was the one who most enjoyed the security of this pack. He liked the business and the money, but he preferred the affection and company of a pretty woman first and foremost. To the dismay of his brothers, this is where he spent most of his energies. It didn't hurt that he was also the most alluring in appearance.

Timoteo always found his validation in the attention he garnered from women. First, his relatives would fall all over him at family gatherings, then his parents' friends would light up when he entered the room, and then women of all kinds just seemed to want to know him. He relished the flirting and the hunt. The frequent conquests were almost anticlimactic. Apparently, while his protectors were serving time, Timoteo attracted the attention of the wrong woman at the precisely the wrong time.

When Timoteo first saw Selena Valdez at a club, he couldn't keep his eyes off of her. She was majestic. Tall and athletically built, long dark hair to her waist with blue eyes and full lips, Selena turned the heads of most men. However, most men didn't look like Timoteo Montenegro. She noticed him first. Her friends told her who and what he was. They tried to warn her, not only for her sake but for his as well. Selena had been spending a lot of time with the leader of the Satanic Saints. The Saints were a ruthless crew operating out of Hunt's Point in the South Bronx. They were very possessive of their territory and their women.

Timoteo and Selena started sneaking around, and word got back to the Saints. Without the protection of his brothers, Timoteo was lured to a meeting by a compromised Selena.

Upon his arrival, Timoteo was brutally beaten by the gang. His lifeless body was left beneath a telephone pole with his dick detached and nailed above his head.

Word got back to his brothers in the pen. They grieved and plotted revenge but were advised that the Saints were too ubiquitous to advance against and too solid of a business partner on several fronts to compromise. Timoteo's dick got him in trouble, and the juice wasn't worth the squeeze for revenge. Tomas, Timoteo's twin, swore to avenge the murder. He blamed himself for being in prison and not being there to offer protection to his wandering-eyed little brother. He was warned not to touch the Saints, but he vowed to find the rat that put him away rendering him unable to protect his baby brother.

Eddy spoke.

"Interesting story, but I don't get the connection."

Eddy could almost hear the smile uncurl on Rappy's face as he responded.

"Esperate, mi amigo."

Rappy continued. Tomas had been released from prison last year. There were rumblings that he had turned the tables on the Feds. Just as they had created an elaborate operation to gather and obtain information against the bad guys, Tomas started to organize a similar network of intelligence to collect information on their sources for the sole purpose of finding the rat. He hired the experts on the dark side to hack, crack, listen, infiltrate, and intimidate the FBI agents involved in his arrest. Leveraging weaknesses among the agents—money, women, or compromising situations—Tomas's black ops team (as he called them) started to hone in on those involved in putting the brothers away.

"So what does that have to do with the shooting?"

"Eddy, I'm putting myself out here, so you need to understand—"

"I get it. Just between you and me, brother."

"You remember how Gordo and his family picked up and moved out real quick?"

"Yeah."

"This happened shortly after his uncle Jackie, his mom's brother, died in an accident at the junk and salvage yard?"

"Yeah."

"Rumor has it that Tomas *arranged* this accident."

"Why? They were related by marriage. Wasn't Jackie married to Tomas's oldest sister, Maria?"

"Si!"

"So it doesn't add up," Eddy said.

"I heard that Jackie used to run some errands for the Doble Doble. He wasn't into the shit they were, but he was useful for quick stuff ... until he wasn't anymore," Rappy explained.

"That's crazy."

"Eddy, you gotta remember, Gordo's mom also lost her other brother, Ramon, I think his name was, to that shit the DD ran. Horse ... smack. They found him in a burnt-out basement some years ago with a needle in his arm."

"Oh, shit!"

"So you add it up. Gordo's mom had a brother who died a drug addict. Her nephew, JC, Jackie's son, became an addict and died of an overdose as well. And to put a cherry on top of it all, her brother, Jackie, while married to a Doble Doble sister, was doing jobs for them ... got sloppy and became expendable—or so the story goes."

"And if memory serves me," Eddy added, "that same Doble Doble sister died of a heart attack—too much tragedy—shortly after her husband, Jackie's, death. And Gordo's family adopted their remaining children, three girls."

"Si."

"So, Gordo's mom flipped on them in revenge and fled the neighborhood with her extended family?"

"That's what I could piece together," Rappy said.

Afraid someone other than Eddy might hear his conspiracy theory, he whispered further, "I think she got fed up with feeling helpless against the drugs. One too many bodies dropped, and she wanted payback."

"That's crazy!"

"Crazy enough to be true," Rappy snapped back.

"Damn! If that's true, why not go into witness protection?" Eddy questioned.

"Rumor was she turned it down because she was carved out during the investigation, and they had enough evidence to leverage the brothers to agree to a deal without needing her to testify. She just provided the road map that the Feds were able to follow and tag the brothers."

"But why not take witness protection?"

"Apparently, she wanted a normal life for her family and her newly adopted girls, and she didn't want to be looking over her shoulder her whole life. She was reassured that those who knew of her involvement were a small and tight circle. So under the guise of moving away from all the violence and tragedy in her life in the Bronx, she left abruptly with her family, never to return."

"Until recently." Eddy finished Rappy's thought.

"Why did she go back?" he wondered further out loud.

"Don't know, but I suspect she heard Tomas and his brothers got out."

Eddy hung up. His mind started running through possible scenarios. As an agent, he'd learned to reconstruct crime scenes and posit on motives and means. He anticipated what his perp might do. The Doble Doble certainly had the resources to gather intel and build their own mosaic to find the snitch. What didn't make sense was Sylvia's return to the old neighborhood. If, in fact, she was the snitch and she suspected Tomas wanted revenge, why run in his direction? Eddy reflected on his conversation with Gordo. A mother's instinct is to protect her young.

Eddy packed quickly, took Coal to a neighbor, and got to bed. He had an early flight and a full day ahead. But Rappy's tale rattled around his brain, and he just couldn't sleep.

WILLY CULLEN

Willy Cullen—not Colon but Cullen from his father's family—was a study in contrasts. His fair skin and green speckled eyes threw people off when he easily broke into Spanish. His Puerto Rican mother married her Irish mailman right after she became pregnant with their only child. She spoke to her son in the Spanish she was raised with until he was five when she split for another gringo. Willy was raised in the South Bronx. He was called 'cat eyes' by us neighborhood kids. He played ball in the streets with us as a youngster before he started his early run with the local gang.

"Hey, cat eyes, we're choosing up sides for a little stickball. Wanna play?" we'd asked.

And he'd respond: "Nah, I got some biz with the fellas to take care of. I'll catch you later."

It seemed easier to boost a couple of car radios and sell a little weed than to go to school, come home to hang with us, and then get whupped by his drunk-ass pops for no reason. Willy's physical strength and early education in criminal activity soon became intimidating to his father, who eventually backed off and asked fewer and fewer questions. Despite his distaste for school, Willy liked to read and was curious enough about the world around him that he snuck off to the library when he thought no one was watching. He read books on travel, took in success stories about athletes and leaders, and applied what he learned to accelerate the arc of his life on the dark side. He was street-smart, self-educated, and constantly conflicted. Life at home was best avoided, and he longed for a sense of belonging. Long after our last little league contest, Willy often told me to thank my pops for coaching the team and buying him a piragua after every game. I can still see him asleep in the back seat of my father's car, a wry smile on his face— *what was he thinking?* —his catcher's equipment soiled and still clinging to his Coke-machine frame. Willy was a rare combo: sensitive, self-aware, and lethal. Mr. Rare Combo moved up the gang ranks quickly. So it was strange that he got pinched late in his career and did a bid at Rikers and even stranger when he suddenly decided to get out of the life shortly after doing his time.

During his stretch at Rikers, Willy got religion. Not religion with Jesus, but hearing his girl had his baby and had moved way upstate for a better life got Willy thinking. He knew he was smart and capable, and having had a mother who vamoosed early in his life and a father who crawled in a bottle soon thereafter motivated him to want to escape this nasty cycle. He had enough scratch stashed away. Coming up, he had found his family in the streets and on the stoops hanging out and scheming together. They planned together and fought together, and it felt good, but where had it all led? They had lived for each day. There was never any talk about tomorrow. All these guys had several kids with different women, and these kids were going to be as fucked up as their parents. Willy knew their absence was as damaging as the violence had been. Willy continued to read in prison. With each passing week, it became clear that what he really wanted was a family. It wouldn't be easy to move on, but didn't every story he read involve obstacles that needed to be overcome before the hero emerged triumphant?

Willy walked out of Rikers and for the next few months planned the details of his move upstate. He never breathed a word of this to a soul. He played along with his gang mates, being careful not to become entangled directly in any activities that could send him back to prison. He shared his prison stories as much to validate his cred as leader as to buy him time to escape. He communicated with his girl in secret and told her that her faith in him was soon to be rewarded.

And one day, Willy "Cat Eyes" Cullen, the leader of the Satanic Saints, just disappeared.

GORDO AND FLACO IN NEW YORK

If you were Puerto Rican and died in the Bronx, you were viewed at Ortiz's Funeral Home and buried at St. Raymond's cemetery. It was an unwritten rule. I'd been to many services at both places over the years. If you were related to the deceased, you'd eventually end up at the Chinese restaurant across the street from Ortiz's. You'd marvel at the Chinese waiters who spoke fluent Spanish. If that weren't strange enough, you could order *comida de barrio* (food of the neighborhood—Puerto Rican fare) while you told stories of the dearly departed between the afternoon and the evening viewings.

On the morning of the funeral, you'd gather at Ortiz's and pray before they loaded the coffin into the hearse. After the church service and before the burial, the hearse would wind its way back to the neighborhood as a final goodbye. The procession would slowly pass by the apartment building of the deceased and sound a horn as a farewell. Neighbors would silently stand outside or hang out of their apartment windows as a final salute. The ride to St. Raymond's Cemetery on the outskirts of the Bronx was long. As you approached the cemetery street, vendors offered flowers to adorn the plots. And there were plots—a whole lot of plots!

That's what struck me most when I went to visit my mother's grave—so many headstones stretching across rolling fields of grass bordered on either side by major thoroughfares. The contrast of the living speeding along in their cars against the stillness of the dead lying silently side by side was almost illogical.

Cemeteries have always fascinated me. You walk through and read the gravestones, which give you names and dates and maybe a little ditty about who is buried beneath; however, by and large, it is left to your imagination to fill in the dash. What exactly happened between their date of birth and their date of death is a mystery to the average wanderer, walker, visitor, stranger, or attendee at another graveside service. Unless the deceased is known to you, there is a story that germinates in your mind as you stare at the dates and names. Your imagination fills in the unknowns that sit between the dates of origin and the dates of demise. What era did they live in? What were their living conditions? You do the math. How old were they when they passed? Why so young? What happened? Why so old? How did they live? Where did they live? Why are they buried here?

It is said that you can tell a lot about a civilization and culture by how they treat their dead. Many cemeteries are marked with stones; others with simpler works; still others have statues, mausoleums, and intricate internment configurations— all in tribute to those who have passed away. St. Raymond's, reflective of its assorted clientele, ran the gamut in decorative configurations for the dead, from the sublime to the garish. Some cemeteries, like clubs, are only for certain members of a community. Sometimes their markers are made uniform to harmonize the importance of each person laid to rest—no one better than the other. This was not the design of this particular cemetery. There were plenty colorful markers that provided a physical location for family and friends to grieve. St. Raymond's was a polyglot of departed citizens who took their turns inhabiting the Bronx from the Irish, Germans, Italians, and Eastern Europeans to the current batch of Caribbeans (Puerto Ricans, Dominicans, Haitians), as well as the Black refugees from down South. Each group had their burial customs, and together, they created a diverse tapestry of burial plots.

Amid the quiet of the dead, I often did my best thinking. Of course, I was there to pay my respects to my mother and other relatives. My father, Jhonny Quintana, felled by cancer, lay beneath my mother's remains. And here was Jackie, my mom's brother, who died suddenly in a work accident. JC, Jackie's son and my mom's nephew, who died young. And finally, there was Maria, Jackie's wife, JC's mom, and my mother's sister-in-law. Some say she died of a broken heart, overcome by the grief of losing both her son and husband so close together. Her ashes were interred in a gravesite next to her son and husband. When Maria died, her three girls became my sisters, adopted and integrated as if they'd always been with us.

I was freshening the flowers and arranging the grass and dirt when the burner buzzed in my pocket. It was Eddy.

"Hermano, we need to talk," he said.

"You got anything?"

"Better to talk face-to-face. Remember Manny's on Westchester Avenue, under the el?"

Manny's was a local neighborhood joint that served beer, mixed drinks, and pizza. My father played for Manny's softball team most Saturdays back in the day. After settling their bets for that day's game, my father and his friends headed to Manny's for drinks and cards. Eddy was drafted to play for the team from time to time when they were in a tight spot—the next best available player and all—the grown-ups covering the teenager's action. I hadn't thought about the place in years, at least not since my pops died some years back and his teammates came to pay their respects.

"Sure. Is it still there?" I asked.

"Yes! I landed, and I need to make one stop before I head over there. See you there in about two hours." Eddy clicked off.

BOBBY CAPORALE

"Bobby, thanks for meeting me on such short notice."

Eddy greeted his old friend as he slipped in across from him in the corner booth furthest from the entrance.

"No problem. An old buddy flies in from his island retreat and says he'd like to pick your brain on a few incidents in my city. No biggie!"

"Gracias."

Bobby Caporale was an old high school rival of Eddy's. They met on the all-city banquet circuit and became fast friends. Bobby went to Xavier in Manhattan. He was a quick-as-shit option quarterback who was perfect for the wishbone offense they ran at his school. If Bobby were a few inches taller, he may have taken his game down to Austin to where the offense originated at the University of Texas. But at less than six feet, Bobby headed to Davidson in North Carolina.

Bobby liked to remind Eddy how tough he was—at Xavier in Manhattan, they practiced on concrete. A knee injury early his sophomore year ended his college football career. He transferred up to John Jay College in New York to study criminal justice. A career soon followed with the NYPD. He quickly climbed the ranks to get his gold shield. Eddy stayed in touch with

Bobby over the years as friends and business associates. They both chased bad guys. Without betraying any confidences, they were able to compare notes and blow off steam. Bobby lived in Douglaston, a nice section of Queens close to LaGuardia Airport and Shea Stadium. They met at a diner near the airport.

"Looks like you managed to keep on the weight," Eddy jabbed.

"Ah, shut the fuck up!" Bobby returned fire and moved the conversation along. "So I asked a buddy downtown to do me a solid on the snatch and grabs from the South Bronx."

"And?"

"I reviewed all three incidents. There were three separate pairs of bad guys on three different crotch rockets. All six were covered head to toe in black: helmets, visors, turtlenecks, gloves, pants, and boots. No skin exposed."

"Interesting."

"None of the vics could identify skin color. They all had different descriptions of the voices—black, Latino, city, whatever that means—"

"The stickup guys spoke?" Eddy questioned.

"Yes and no," Bobby began. "Each victim stated that they did not say much other than to demand the phone. And one victim swore it was not a guy but a woman's voice. And there were several witnesses who said they heard the shooter yell something at your buddy's mother, but none could say with any certainty what that was."

"The first two were treated as robberies and the last a murder, correct?" Eddy replied seeking confirmation

"Yes, but the trail went cold fast. No one has identified the shooter. The incidents were in three different locations, and the surveillance and security cameras in each area caught nothing!"

"License plates?"

"Each bike had those anti photo film covers that obscure the plates in any photos or videos. Even enhancement technology couldn't sharpen the image."

"Anything unusual about the bikes?"

"All mass-market, three different manufacturers, and no distinctive markings or features."

"How about the gun?"

"All three events featured a gun being waved in the face of our vics. The bullets recovered from your buddy's mom were from a .45 semiautomatic. There was a ghost gun, a .45, found in a dumpster ten blocks away from the shooting. The markings matched the gun to your shooting. No prints on the weapon, no serial number, untraceable."

"Man. These guys are smart. Good. Calculated." Eddy mused.

"Eddy, you really believe these were orchestrated to set up a hit?"

"That's my working theory."

"Well, whoever you think did this was careful in their planning," Bobby nodded as he spoke. "They must have known something about the workings of the NYPD in the South Bronx. The series of robberies hid their true intent. This fatal incident was disposed of and characterized quickly by the local boys in blue. The shooting was thought to be random and an unfortunate outcome of a robbery gone bad."

"It's not their fault. If I'm correct, that's exactly what this plot was banking on—assumptions by NYPD based on prior bad acts in the neighborhood. That's the reason why—" *They had to lure her down here*, Eddy thought to himself. He didn't finish his thought out loud, being careful not to reveal too much. They needed their prey on their turf. If they went hunting in Connecticut, there might be too many questions.

"Sorry I couldn't be of more help," Bobby intoned.

"You did just fine."

"Not much to go on."

"True, but it is all too convenient. Three different pairs with three different bikes, all for an iPhone or two? Seems like a lot of theater for such a small take. It's not like they were grabbing diamonds, pearls, and cash from their victims."

"You want me to do anything else?" Bobby asked.

"Nah, I'm good," Eddy said. "Thank you, tough guy. I owe you one!"

Bobby walked away, actually limped away—old football injury and all—from his meeting with Eddy with a shitty feeling. Each of the three snatch and grabs were identical except the scream and the shooting with the last victim. Careful not to arouse too much attention, Bobby had read the notes on the cases online and relayed what he'd learned to Eddy. However, he knew from experience that there might be some things said to the patrolmen on the scene that seemed inconsequential at the time but was important in the overall picture, yet would never make it to the record. Bobby had indeed reached out to the patrolman who was the first to arrive on the scene.

"I just had a few questions on that snatch and grab that went south," Bobby asked the officer.

"Shoot!"

"The notes on the case say that the perps pulled up as they had in the prior two instances, grabbed the phone, yelled something, and shot the victim."

"Yeah, that's right."

"None of the witnesses could identify the shooters because of the head-to-toe black clothing, but did anybody hear what was shouted prior to the shooting?" Bobby asked.

The patrolman hesitated just a beat. "Have you talked to my sergeant?"

"Why do I need to talk to your sergeant? I'm asking you. You were there. Did anyone report hearing what was shouted?"

"Ah, yes someone did come forward with what they believe they heard, but ..."

"But what?"

"Sarge told us to leave it out of the report because it made no sense."

"What did they shout?"

"I'm a little uncomfortable here, Detective," the officer continued to deflect. "I don't want to disobey my sarge."

"If it made no sense, what's the harm in sharing?" Bobby asked. "I'm just looking into this for a friend."

"Geronimo!"

"Geronimo?"

"Yeah, that's what the witness thought they heard. Ya know, like when you jump off a high place, you yell, 'Geronimo!'"

"You're right. That makes no sense." Bobby agreed.

"See."

"Did the witness say they yelled it just like that? 'Geronimo.'?"

"Well, she wasn't really sure. She thought it was 'for Geronimo,' which also makes no sense. So that's why I think the sarge thought it was garbage."

"Hm. OK. Thanks," Eddy said.

"Sure thing."

After the meeting with the patrolman, Bobby had received a text from a private number. It read: "Stick to the script. Relay only what was in the report."

The message was accompanied by a few pictures, all taken from a distant vantage point, of his wife at the supermarket and his daughter on her college campus. Judging from the weather and their clothing, Bobby knew the pictures had been taken recently. After he read the text and viewed the pictures, the bubbles telling him the sender was typing another message again started to erupt.

"Cepeda is your friend. They are your family. You choose."

Bobby, normally brave and unflappable, was shaken. Whoever the sender was knew that he was looking into this matter for a friend—a friend named Cepeda. Eddy had told him that he had a theory that this was a revenge hit ordered by Tomas Montenegro as pay back for the brothers' incarceration and his twin's murder while he was away—his twin, Timoteo.

Geronimo? Could it have been 'for Timoteo?' Bobby wondered.

Bobby liked Eddy. He was good people and a fellow officer of the law, but he wasn't family. Whoever was sending the texts also had a line into the department causing the sergeant to quash this information. *Eddy will get there on his own*, Bobby reasoned. He hadn't exactly lied when he told him what he had read in the reports, but he still felt really shitty about omitting this tidbit.

CONFESSIONAL

"It's dark in here."

"It is always dark in the heart of Satan, my son."

Right on cue when the portal to the confessional door slid open, the confessor stated the key words for identification, soon to be met by a confirmation that he was communicating with his proper contact.

Bobby had set this sequence of call and reply many years ago with his special confidential informant. He summoned the CI to this agreed-upon meeting spot by placing a pair of red Chuck Taylor Converse All-Stars over a low-hanging telephone wire just outside this very church. The CI had to go by this church to visit his mother every Tuesday; therefore, he would know he was being called to a meet the next day, early morning, inside the third confession box on the left at St. Athanasius Catholic Church in the South Bronx. If it was urgent, requiring a meet that same day, the Chuck Taylor sneakers would be the color green.

Striking a bargain with the local priest, along with a generous annual donation, Bobby had keys to the church to use at his discretion.

"Father, you save souls inside this church. I can save lives outside this church if you allow me to hear confessions with a select group of our flock occasionally."

Bobby was so charming and persuasive when he needed to be; he always thought he should have gone to law school. In fact, he negotiated the cooperation of this CI many years ago by burying the name of this guy's younger brother in connection to a large drug bust. The kid was a minor player in the food chain, but when Bobby heard who he was related to, he jumped on the opportunity to broker a deal. The kid was the youngest brother of a major gang member whose mother had anointed the child as the last hope to break the cycle of crime and poverty. She believed he was a prince destined for college and greatness, unlike her older boys. Big brother was very protective of his brother, and more so of his mother. He didn't want her heart broken any further and wanted to relieve her of any undue worry. Bobby offered the elixir to her suffering if only big brother confessed his sins from time to time. Thus was born a deal between Papo, the number-two man of the Satanic Saints, and Bobby Caporale. Whenever Bobby needed intel from the street, he hung the sneakers.

Bobby looked at Papo through the mesh screen. He had him in side profile. Papo's hands were stitched together as if in prayer, held in front of his mouth right below his nose. He looked contemplative, with his forehead furrowed and his eyes gazing downward. Bobby noticed the small scars along Papo's neck behind his ears, the dirt beneath his fingernails, and the gnarly mashup of his fingers. This guy had lived a hundred lifetimes.

"Padre, you rang?" Papo questioned.

"Yes."

"What's up?"

"You hearing anything about Tomas Montenegro since his release from prison?" Bobby asked.

Papo slowly turned his head toward the voice on the other side of the screen. He squinted his eyes to focus on Bobby, all the while chewing the nail of one thumb as though mulling how to answer the question.

"Why you asking?"

"He fucking threatened my family, that's why," Bobby explained. Papo muffled a laugh into his hand.

"You think that's funny?"

"Nah. Ironic is all."

"Why ironic?"

Papo lit a cigarette and took in a long pull before answering. He tipped the burning ash off the end of the cigarette and rubbed it into the right knee of his dirty jeans.

Bobby reminded him that there was no smoking inside the church.

"It's a fire code violation. Besides, smoking in a confessional is like teasing God to send you to hell."

Papo choked on smoke as he laughed at that last comment.

"Bro, I'm going to hell one way or another. It's just a matter of when. It don't matter if I smoke or not, but I'm OK with that. I've done what I've had to do to survive. No regrets."

Bobby shook his head from side to side either from impatience with Papo's meandering or in wonderment over Papo's rationalization of his life choices. He had no doubt that Papo's ecosystem was calibrated differently than his own, and he was somewhat sympathetic given the circumstances, but they were still choices and decisions that Papo made that Bobby could not fathom making.

"What about Tomas is ironic?" Bobby asked again.

"Dude's a scary motherfucker. He and his crew control just about everything round here, as I'm guessing you know. He threatens a lot of people, and I guess it's not just the bad guys anymore but now cops like you too. He don't give a shit who he hurts. Tomas is a control freak. He likes things tight. And I understand he's cleaning up shit that he couldn't while he was away. What'd you do to deserve his attention?"

"My job!"

Another muffled snicker.

"Your job must have gotten in the way of Tomas's business," Papo replied rather quickly.

"Papo, what are you hearing?"

"Listen, man. I feel for you. I do. I don't know anything, but the Saints do business with the Doble Doble from time to time. A while back, we may have done something that he didn't approve of, and he couldn't control the situation—that is, until now. It was payback in our eyes, but he may have seen it differently. My boss is missing, and it ain't no coincidence that he's gone since Tomas got out."

Bobby was silent for a time. Papo was motionless as well. Bobby put his face in his hands and let out a long breath.

"Listen, man. Tomas is pretty black and white," Papo said trying to advise Bobby. "Not that you want to know what I think, but whatever it is that he or his people have asked you to do—or not do—you should go along. He's fearless. He doesn't give a shit about consequences except for those he hands out himself."

"What about your boss—Willy 'Cat Eyes,' right?"

"That's our problem. We made our bed—" Papo didn't finish the thought but transitioned to another.

"Listen, Tomas keeps score. He believes in the old shit—an eye for an eye, blood for blood. No disrespect, but you can't

49

afford to lose either. In the streets, that's how the Saints play. We know the rules. We play by them. We own the consequences. You, not so much."

"I'm not scared of that scumbag!"

"It don't matter, man. It's like when I was a kid and trying to act big and bad on the street to get some cred. You'd get in someone's face and tell them that if they throw the first punch they better kill you because if they don't you're going to fuck them up real good. Well, that's Tomas for real. Don't throw a punch at him if you don't intend to kill him because he'll fuck you—or anyone you care about—real bad!"

Through the screen partition, Papo saw Bobby Caporale get up and make the sign of the cross while he uttered his closing phrase before exiting the box.

"Go and sin no more."

MANNY'S

Manny's was the same—dark and dank with the stale smell of spilt beer. The aroma from the pizza oven struggled to cover the stench. It was a large metallic structure that took up the back half of the bar. Its doors opened and shut many times over the course of the day and well into the night, receiving and dispensing large pies spread with the usual cheese and sauce. Pizza came in only one size here, very large, but you could add anything from the conventional, like pepperoni, mushrooms, and onions, to the exotic, like shrimp, pineapple, morcilla, and even a spread of mofongo. The bar business was dwarfed by the pizza business. I saw Eddy tucked into a booth with his back against the wall facing out to see all incoming traffic, a residual habit from his former life. El Gran Combo de Puerto Rico was playing on Manny's sound system. The rhythmic timbales, conga drums, and piano syncopated, inviting the listener to sway down the aisle to a seat. The ping, ping of the cowbell and bleat of the brass just added to the island symphony. The dark cavern of Manny's place was warm with a Latin vibe. Eddy got up and hugged me with a kiss on the cheek and a couple of pats on the back.

"My man, it's amazing how you haven't changed over the years."

"Eddy, don't be playing me," I told him. "My hair is in retreat. I get up in the morning in sections, like a question mark unfolding. Plus, you just saw me a little while back at my mom's services. Asshole!"

Eddy laughed. His eyes, with the lightest crinkle, smiled. He was the one who had not changed. He was tight and taut in all the right places, and he looked like he could still knock a running back on his ass. We ordered, me a Corona with lime and Eddy a Cuba libre. For old time's sake, we added a pizza with chunks of morcilla and dollops of mofongo. Eddy got down to business.

"Gordo, I knew your moms pretty well, and she was always pretty good to me, but I need you to fill me in on the family history," Eddy started in immediately.

"I don't understand."

"I made some calls, and there may be something to your *theory*."

"Really?" I asked.

"I haven't pieced it all together, but something doesn't add up. I think there's history with your people and some bad people."

"The Montenegro—"

Eddy cut me off, leaned in, grabbed my collar, and told me to lower my voice.

"Si," he whispered. "I talked to a couple of people from the old neighborhood and asked a favor or two from former colleagues."

Eddy has been busy these last twenty-four hours, I thought.

"And what did you hear?"

Eddy leaned into my ear.

"It's not only what I heard but also some things I read in the files of my former employer." Eddy paused. "The files talk about a critical informant in the Doble Doble takedown. They only refer to this person as *familiar* to the Doble Doble."

"So? That could mean a lot of things, Eddy."

"Does the name Mari Diaz mean anything to you?" he asked.

"I don't think so," I told him. "Why?"

"That name appeared in quotes a few times in the files around this DD thing."

"Wait. Wasn't she the woman who used to live in the basement apartment of our building? You know, the one with the good-looking daughter ... You remember, she used to walk her daughter to school and back every day until almost high school?"

"Oh yeah. What ever happened to them?" Eddy asked.

"I think they moved out to Queens around the same time my family moved north. Interesting ..."

"In any case, your family goes *way* back with the Montenegros. Your grandparents and your uncles knew them back in the day. The roots go deep into your mom's family's life, right? I need you to give me a history lesson."

"How far back?" I asked.

"Let's start with tus abuelos, your mom's parents, Caridad and Diego, right?"

CARIDAD, FEBRUARY 5, 1920

It was a balmy Thursday in San Juan—the kind of day where the sky is blue, but the air is languid, filled with moisture that envelops you from your ankles and ties up around your hair. Caridad Colon had risen very early in her aunt's home—a lean-to of loose boards, ill-fitting windows, and a dirt floor—that morning just outside of the city in Santurce for her final trek to the port. It had been a long journey with her younger brother, Santos. They left their overcrowded home—eight kids, two rooms—in Bayamon days before, headed to the Port of San Juan to journey on to New York. Caridad had heard the streets were paved with gold.

Caridad's mother, Aquilina, sent her oldest and youngest children for the better life extolled in letters sent by her cousins from the mainland. At eighteen, Caridad was tall, willowy, and lovely. With long, wavy, dark-caramel-colored hair, hazel eyes, and honey-hued skin, she was just becoming aware how her presence changed a room. Aquilina taught her daughter all the important domestic skills but suspected that Caridad had grown curious about the world beyond their kitchen, and the world was starting to notice her child with a little *too* much curiosity.

Sewing what money she could spare inside her daughter's dress and handing her daughter a small wooden crucifix, Aquilina prayed over her children while giving them strict instructions on navigating their journey. Fearful that they might get separated, she tied the end of a small rope to Caridad's wrist and tied the other end to five-year-old Santo's belt. Aquilina knew that sending them to New York was a big risk but necessary. Because she could not afford passage for all her children, she selected the strongest and the most meek to venture out first, knowing that the one would take care of the other. She believed that each end of the birth spectrum represented hope.

Caridad hated being tethered to Santos but understood the responsibility. She liked the way the crucifix felt in her hands. Smoothing her thumb over the coarse wood in the pocket of her dress gave her comfort. It gave her a sense of purpose and served as her talisman as she braved the muddied streets and throngs of people headed to the pier. The *Philadelphia* was an old passenger ship, certainly seaworthy but tired, rusted, and groaning, protesting its leash to the dock. Caridad and Santos stared up at this huge metal boat that was to take them across the ocean for a few days. It was to transport them to a new life filled with ... more. If Caridad was frightened, she gave no hint. She leaned into the plank leading up to the deck and marched ahead, pulling her younger charge gently behind her.

They arrived in New York in a few days. The voyage was rough, the seas rolling the *Philadelphia* as it departed the warm climes of the Caribbean and entered the less hospitable and chilly waters of the Northeast. Caridad and Santos huddled against one another the whole trip to ward off the winter winds. They wore only the clothes of sunny Puerto Rico. It was so cold in New York that the ship's captain took them inside the dock's offices at the port and wrapped them in blankets until someone came to claim them. Aquilina's cousins, Manuel and Isabel, finally arrived and hugged the children tightly. They laughed aloud at both the crucifix and the rope, and they were taken aback by the beautiful young woman Caridad had become.

It took several buses and subways to bring them uptown to the East Side apartment. Filled with generous portions of arroz con pollo, the siblings fell soundly asleep folded into one another on a couch covered by a quilt. The next morning, Isabel spoke to them both about what was expected of them in their new life. Caridad, with Isabel's help, would find a job as a seamstress in one of the many clothing factories downtown, while Santos would attend school in the fall. Because neither child spoke English, Isabel told them she and Manual would teach them what they'd learned. Caridad knew it was up to her to make the most of every opportunity she'd be given.

She found work the first day. Isabel taught her how to take the subway to and from the factory. It accelerated the English lessons. She tried to instill some city smarts into the young woman.

"Not everyone is your friend, mija. Entiendes?" Isabel warned.

"Si, tia."

Caridad was soon making enough money to help her cousins with the apartment and send some home to her mother, and this is how her life started in New York.

DIEGO, 1923

Diego Cruz was a scrapper. At nineteen, he was lean and sinewy, tanned and sculpted—the result of many hours of work. Born and raised in a small village with a working harbor at the foot of a large hill in Cuba, he was in constant demand for his strong back and his indomitable determination. There was always something someone was willing to pay him to do whether in dinero or arroz—money or rice. At the end of most days, Diego stood at the docks and stared out at the sea, wondering what else was out there. While his friends often spent hours playing dominoes and drinking beer in the local dives near the docks, he would sit with his legs dangling off the pier, his thoughts swirling around like the cigar smoke that encircled his head and moved slowly skyward. He pulled on his cigar slowly and dreamed. He dreamed of life beyond Cuba. He wanted to go to New York. He heard there was much work there for someone who was not afraid of hard work, and they paid in cash, not rice.

"Diego, why you always down here smoking your cigars and looking out at the sea? No cerveza and chicas out there, hermano!" Chino, Diego's best friend, asked.

"It's peaceful down here. Quiet," answered Diego.

"Silencio. Is that what you want? Lucia has been asking for you, compadre! She don't want no quiet, papi!"

"Chino, you ever think about what's outside this village? You ever wonder what other Lucias are out there? What ..." Diego's voice trailed off to a contemplative whisper, not completing his query.

"I'm good here. My family, my friends ... It's simple. I wake up, work, drink, eat, and chase the pretty girls. What else is there?"

Diego knew right then that he needed to move from dreaming to planning. Chino's rationale was not unusual for his village. It was not good or bad, but it was just not big enough for Diego. He was curious, and he was willing to take a chance on something new—something different. The next day Diego left for Havana.

With his easy smile and good manners, he found work almost immediately as a cabin boy aboard a small cruise ship that set sail for Miami and New York on a regular rotating basis. Diego cleaned cabins and fetched sundries for the monied passengers aboard the ship. He was polite and diligent in his duties. It earned him compliments and the occasional tip. The work suited him, and he absorbed all the sounds and sights on his travels to and from the mainland. He noticed everything from how the men carried themselves, their attire, their grooming, and their diction to how they interacted with women and the staff. Diego noted that the most generous with time and money were also those who didn't seem eager to impress and didn't need to draw a distinction between themselves and the help. When he felt he had learned all he could, he planned to jump ship at the next New York docking. He had family in the city.

Federico Ayala was Diego's boss aboard the cruise line. He was a round fellow with red cheeks and a deep baritone voice who never missed a meal or turned down a drink. Educated enough to move easily from Spanish to English, Fed was an affable man, fair and quick with a contagious laugh. Federico spoke to Diego in their native tongue.

"Diego, Mr. Arturo has requested that you attend to his cabin on his upcoming trip to Miami."

"Miami?" Diego inquired with a surprise in his voice that he didn't intend to reveal.

"Problemo?"

"No, no, Jefe! It's just that I was scheduled to do the New York trips this month," Diego lamented.

"Si, pero, Señor Arturo is an important passenger who seems to like what you do for him and his family, and his business takes him to Miami, not New York."

"Jefe, como no." Diego sullenly agreed with his boss.

He had finally summoned the courage to act and was rattled by this new development. He liked Señor Arturo. He was one of the generous and kind passengers. Diego really liked waiting on the man. Arturo never summoned or ordered him, he asked with genuine inquiry, and always thanked him as though his duties were a favor to him and not a job. While not exactly sure of the source of his wealth, Diego believed Arturo was somehow involved with the sugar cane or rum trade. His travels took him to Miami often, either alone or in the company of one of his young sons. Normally, being requested by such a gentleman would make Diego's day. Now, he let out a long sigh. He knew he'd have to summon the courage once again in the future to jump ship at some unknown time.

It was a bright June morning when Señor Arturo boarded. Don Rafael, his ten-year-old son, was in tow that morning. Diego greeted them warmly and pressed a freshly baked *pan de aqua* that he picked up in the galley into the young boy's hand, but only after getting the nod of approval from his father. Diego put on his bravest face and projected his biggest smile as he ushered them both into their cabin while hauling their luggage.

Despite Diego's best efforts, Señor Arturo sensed something was off. While tugging at Diego's sleeve, Arturo jutted out his chin and lifted his eyebrows in a gesture of both concern and inquiry.

"Que paso, mi amigo?"

Reluctant at first, Diego turned his eyes downward. Slowly, he returned Arturo's gaze.

"Señor, you have been good to me, and I am honored, as always, that you would request my services"—he hesitated, unsure of how much he should share— "but I was hoping for the New York trip ... because ..." He paused, stumbling over his words. "I was going to jump ship to stay in New York."

If Arturo was surprised, he didn't show it. He nodded his head and stuck out his lower lip in contemplative approval. What he said next stunned Diego, causing him to tilt his head slightly to make sure he heard and understood his patron's words.

"I will help you," Arturo said. He then asked Diego if he had people in New York. He did. Did he know where they lived? Yes. How would he reach them once he arrived at port? He wasn't sure, but he recently looked at a map of New York to determine how far the port was from where his relations lived. It wasn't that far, or at least Diego thought he was resourceful enough to figure it out.

When they docked in Miami, Arturo asked his local people to take care of his son for the afternoon. Slipping the captain of the ship a few bucks, Arturo told him that he needed Diego to assist him with some tasks for the next few days. Properly greased, the captain made no objections. With Diego following in his wake, Arturo made some inquiries on the dock in Miami regarding any boat that was headed to New York. In whispered conversations and a furtive handshake filled with a few dollars, Arturo secured passage for Diego.

"Diego, this man will take you on this boat to New York, but you have to work on deck as your payment for the trip," Arturo explained.

Diego was elated. He hugged Arturo. The patron, although surprised, returned the hug and then held the young man at arm's length by the shoulders.

"Mijo, make the most of your new life!"

That evening, Diego could hardly sleep. It felt like Christmas Eve. He had a few moments of panic. All his recent actions were impulsive. Diego paused to scribble two letters. Although not formally schooled, he had some rudimentary writing skills. The first was to his family back in Cuba to inform them that he was no longer in Havana but heading to New York to start a new life. The second was to his uncle in New York. Benito was Diego's father's youngest brother. He had left Cuba shortly after Diego's father died from illness. Benito was quite fond of Diego and sensed that he, like himself, was bigger than the island of their birth. He often sent his young nephew postcards from New York. Diego had cut out the return address from one such postcard and put it in his wallet many years ago, almost as a silent pledge to himself to journey to New York one day. Diego wrote to Benito with his plans and the name of his ship coming in from Miami. He hoped that his uncle would receive the letter in time and be waiting for him at the Port of New York.

The ship arrived one morning after some hard days at sea. Diego, used to physical labor, was nonetheless overwhelmed by the amount of work required by ship hands to get the vessel from one port to another. He lifted and hauled many items around and under the deck. He worked as the sun rose in the horizon until it ducked in behind the ship's wake. His clothes were dark with sweat and grease. His face was tanned and darkened with stubble. He was so tired that he thought he felt both the groan of his muscles and heard the crackling of his joints and bones. He was quite a sight as he came down the plank onto the dock where his uncle Benito stood smiling.

"Sobrino, aqui!" Benito shouted to his nephew to let him know he was there. "Diego, you look tired."

Somehow Diego thought his arrival would be more ceremonial—the family scion arriving triumphantly on these shores, clean and neat. Instead, he looked like a stowaway who had been holed up on a ship during a rough passage, which he just now realized he had been.

"Tio, you got my letter. Thank you for coming to meet me. I'm sorry I just laid this on you."

"Esta bien. No problem. Let's get you home."

They gathered up the duffel bag that Diego had dragged from Cuba to Miami and now to New York and headed uptown to an apartment building. Diego quickly bathed in the tub in the kitchen and ate several bowls of rice, beans, and platanos. He fell into a deep sleep on the cot his uncle set aside for him near the only fan in the apartment. Diego finally relaxed.

The next day, Benito took Diego with him to his job downtown at the Plaza Hotel. Benito worked in the kitchen doing odds and ends for the chef and his crew. He worked hard and was well thought of in and around the kitchen. Benito introduced Diego to the head chef and served as translator as they went back and forth about anything that his nephew could do in the kitchen for a job. Diego told Benito, who told the chef, that he worked the docks in his Cuban village and was very familiar with fish. He also shared his exploits of hauling fruit and vegetables from the farms onto the local ships and into the restaurants in his village. He rounded out his many examples of hard work with his service as a cabin boy in Havana. During this narrative, the chef, a man in his fifties with a ruddy complexion, rough hands, and wrinkles that attested to his age and experience, nodded his head as he folded his arms across his generous torso.

"Benito, why should I hire your nephew? He doesn't speak any English. You may not speak much, but you speak enough."

Benito turned to Diego with concern and related in Spanish the objection his boss had just registered.

Diego nodded his head slowly up and down and then in rapid Spanish emphatically said to Benito, "Tell your boss the less I talk, the more I work!"

"*Que?*"

"Tell him. The less I talk, the more I work!"

Benito turned to the chef, and not knowing how he'd react to his nephew's clever response, he just repeated it word-for-word.

"Chef, my nephew says the less he talks, the more he works." And not feeling sure this brash response was appropriate enough, he added, "And he'll learn English quickly."

The next day Diego was cleaning and cutting vegetables in the kitchen of the Plaza Hotel.

CARIDAD AND DIEGO, 1930

Caridad and Diego met at a dance at the Park Palace in East Harlem in 1930. It was one of the hottest dance clubs for Latinos in the city. People went to blow off steam and have a couple of drinks along with a few cigarettes or a cigar, and if they were lucky, they found love (in the moment or more permanently) while swaying to a guaracha, bopping to a charanga, or cozying up during a bolero.

Caridad didn't get out often. She had a son at home now but no husband. Diego too rarely ventured out after long hours in the kitchen, but there was something about this night that beckoned both of them to East Harlem. Caridad was two years older than Diego, but that was not a deterrent to him, and neither was her having a child. He found her enchanting. The moment he saw her in the crowd, he was breathless, and when she asked him for a light near the bathroom, he couldn't believe his luck.

After a hectic, passionate courtship, they married. Caridad soon bore Diego a son, Joaquin, whom they called Jackie, and then another, Ramon, three years later. Soon after, Caridad had her only daughter, my mother, Sylvia.

SYLVIA, BORN 1935

My mother's family lived in the Barrio on 110th Street between Madison and Park avenues—Spanish Harlem. Sylvia had three brothers. Ricky, her half brother from her mother's first marriage, was so much older that she had few memories of him. Jackie, older by five years, took to the streets quickly and seemed to come in and out of the apartment only to satisfy his basic needs of food and shelter. Ramon, on the other hand, was very close to his sister; thus, she loved her brother Ramon deeply.

Manual and Isabel, Caridad's mother's cousins, lived around the block and had started a family of their own, so Sylvia had many cousins in the neighborhood. The families did many things together and spent every holiday visiting one another. Caridad's mother and father, Sylvia's grandparents, had joined the clan in New York, and their nearby apartment became the center of most celebrations. These few square blocks in Spanish Harlem soon became the loving village—the epicenter of Sylvia's young life. She was content and happy.

As a child, Sylvia admired her mother. In her she saw a strong, attractive, and independent woman—a woman whose beauty belied her grit and determination. A rebel, Caridad was the only woman in her neighborhood to walk down the street in tightly cinched pants, a man-tailored shirt, and flats with a cigarette hanging from her painted lips with the kind of swagger that evoked both envy and admiration. She worked full time until Diego told her that he could make enough so she could stay home. Still, she took in piecework from the neighbors in order to keep busy, keep her skills as a seamstress sharp, and pocket a little of her own money. Caridad was kind and caring to her family. She told them stories about the boogeyman and fairy tales and actually had Sylvia believing that Santa Claus lived right around the corner. Caridad went so far as to point out the building and his windows, with the shades drawn, to her incredulous offspring.

In 1941 Caridad and Diego moved to the Bronx. This was a big move, as they were finally moving out of El Barrio and onto a better life. Everyone from the neighborhood was impressed, especially Sylvia. She felt important and special. It was a clear and warm summer day when they moved to 162nd Street and Prospect Avenue. To her, she felt like she had moved to the country. Their new apartment was on the top floor of a six-story building. It was spacious and sunny with a lot of windows and expansive views of the groomed, tree-lined concourse below. Where she once shared a room with Ramon, now Sylvia felt like a princess because she had her own space.

Soon the rest of the clan followed her family to the Bronx. Sylvia's grandparents moved around the corner, while Manuel and Isabel bought one of the few private homes on the avenue. Knowing no one else who owned their own home, Sylvia presumed her cousins were rich.

Sylvia and Ramon had daily chores to attend to when they came home from school. Caridad, while not strict, did expect some order around her household. Clean dishes, folded laundry, and dusted tables and lamps—Sylvia and Ramon traded duties and competed against one another to see who could finish fastest and get a word of approval from their mother. They fought from time to time but laughed more often than not. When their mother was otherwise occupied, they got silly and chased each other around the apartment just to hear their laughter echo off the walls. As siblings, they were giddy, goofy, relaxed, and comfortable in each other's company. Sylvia and Ramon were each other's best friend. Jackie tolerated them. They were just being babies, while he was practically a man.

These early years were wonderful for Sylvia. She and Ramon played in the streets and haunted the local candy store every day. When she was twelve and Ramon thirteen, Diego took them both to Cuba for the summer, leaving his wife and oldest son back in New York. Having recently achieved his US citizenship, Diego wanted to show his youngest children the land of his birth while introducing them to his family back home. It was magic! It seemed as though they were suspended in time away from the hustle of New York. Sylvia thought they could stay forever, but soon the peace was shattered with news that Caridad's parents died in a fire, the tragedy summoning them back to reality.

It was a great loss to the family. Their center had dropped into a sinkhole. Darkness seemed to envelope the neighborhood. The mourning process seemed to be a daily struggle, especially for Caridad. Perhaps to fill the void, she decided to go back to work. It seemed to strengthen her and helped her clear the shadows that loomed after the loss. Diego threw himself into work. He worked long hours as it was but seemed to extend his time in the kitchen at the Plaza. His work ethic was appreciated, and he was getting more responsibilities along with the extra hours. Increasingly, he stayed overnight at the hotel once or twice a week. It was rare that he took time off, and when he was home, he sank into the couch with Sylvia and Ramon tucked beneath his strong arms. Sylvia missed him on the nights he came home long after she had gone off to bed, but especially on the nights he didn't come home at all.

"Papi, are you coming home tonight?" Sylvia asked most days as her father headed off to work.

"Necesito trabajar por el jefe."

Diego exclaimed his need to take a shift for his boss to his distraught daughter, who didn't understand his intermittent absences. Slowly, Diego and Caridad saw the clouds clear at home. While Caridad and Diego were operating on different schedules, when they were together, they insisted on living their lives out loud and making memories for their children. Sylvia relished the memories almost as much as she pined for her father when he was gone. Aside from special days, like her birthday, he seemed to be gone more than he was home during the week.

Caridad made sure that she and Diego explored the world outside of the Bronx for their family. They took the kids to many of the local beaches on Long Island and Brooklyn. They went to Coney Island and City Island. They visited swimming pools, amusement parks, and even airports to watch the planes take off and land. Sylvia and Ramon loved it. Jackie participated reluctantly and sullenly. Sylvia thought she was the envy of all the kids on her block. Her mom and dad were rarely home at the same time, but when they were, it seemed they made the most of it. She and her family seemed to enjoy the freedom and simple pleasures of a good life—as good a life as a young girl could imagine.

Caridad was proud but very protective of her daughter. Having great facility on the sewing machine, Caridad could fashion all manner of clothing for her daughter. Inventive enough to look at magazine spreads and advertisements for women's clothing, Caridad replicated blouses, skirts, and dresses for her teenage daughter without the aid of patterns. As Sylvia's young body matured and started filling out, her mother's fashion choices for her daughter, while current, became more conservative. Caridad was very restrictive in allowing Sylvia out on the streets alone. She outlined geographical boundaries for her daughter's life and insisted Sylvia respect them.

SYLVIA AND RAMON, 1950

By the time Sylvia was fifteen, Jackie had already left the apartment, marrying Maria Montenegro—his childhood sweetheart—at nineteen. They started a family of their own with a recently born baby boy they named Juan Carlos, whom they called JC. Diego's hard work and long hours had paid dividends, and he rose through the hierarchy in the Plaza's kitchen, eventually replacing his boss, the retiring head chef. Hilton Hotels, the corporate owner of the Plaza, was opening a luxury hotel in Puerto Rico and asked Diego to command the kitchen duties in their new property. The family agreed that Diego should go ahead alone to Puerto Rico to secure living quarters for them and then send for them once the matter was settled. He left New York with much fanfare and the blessings of his wife and kids.

Caridad awaited word from Diego for several weeks, but nothing came. One of her friends mentioned that she might want to go to Puerto Rico to make sure everything was all right. Caridad left for Puerto Rico and was gone for a little over a week. When she returned, Caridad was broken. The light in her eyes had dulled, the bounce in her step replaced by a shuffle. She was short on details to her family but made it clear that her husband, their father, was not coming back home, and they were not going to Puerto Rico. He was not dead, just unavailable. They had lost him forever.

Diego's desertion changed everything. He had made a good living and provided the small luxuries that Sylvia and her family had come to enjoy. More than the material things, Diego was part of the solid foundation that he and Caridad provided to their family. The earth had suddenly shifted beneath Caridad, and she was having a hard time accepting her new reality. Sylvia and Ramon were also stunned by the rupture in the family and suffered from the fallout of their mother's unnerving.

As Sylvia adored Ramon, Ramon adored his father. Ramon had been a shining light in Diego's eyes. They wrestled on the floor when Diego returned home late from work. Diego took Ramon with him to the kitchen at the Plaza from time to time. He enjoyed the irony of having his young son cut vegetables as he once did. As Caridad sought to make memories for the family, Diego had unintentionally done the same for Ramon. Feeling the sting of his father's surprise departure, Ramon was angry. Upset, confused, and having nowhere to exorcise his demons at home, Ramon retreated more and more to the streets around the neighborhood and beyond the geographical boundaries that his mother had set for Sylvia. He found distraction in the wrong people and withdrew from Sylvia and his mother. While Jackie was upset as well, he had his own family to worry about. Soon enough, Ramon started staying out all night, drinking, and then experimenting with drugs. Eventually, Ramon's ire consumed him, and he succumbed to the numbing weightlessness of heroin. Sylvia was too much of a coward to experiment with anything. While angry as well, she was too worried about her mother's ever-growing distance and brewing wrath. She had also seen what drugs did to people in and around the neighborhood.

Caridad's self-pity led her to be less attentive to her children. Manuel and Isabel came around to check on Caridad and see if the kids needed anything. They tried to console Caridad and encouraged her to soldier on without much success. Money was tight, so Manuel slipped Caridad a few dollars, but Ramon, in the grips of junkie life, stole from his family whatever and whenever he could, negating any financial help his uncle provided.

Ramon was a ghost of himself with few remnants of the boy Sylvia loved. She saw glimpses of his sweetness, but they were overtaken by the darkness of his addiction. Sylvia pained for him. She loved him but abhorred his weakness. Sad, she was disgusted by her mother's inability to feel anything, to do anything, and to merely exist without caring about herself or her children. Sylvia didn't recognize her. The strong woman she once worshipped was gone. Now she only saw an empty soul—a lifeless light. She felt disgusted and cheated at the same time. Sylvia toggled between the betrayal she felt from her father and the distaste she had for her mother.

Ramon saw the emptiness and apathy too. He used it as an opportunity to lash out at Caridad, blaming her for their father's actions and the embarrassment it brought upon them. He fought with his mother constantly, took advantage of her weakness, abused her, and stole whatever he could. He was combative with Sylvia, but she fought back. Ramon was driven by his anger, and like a predator in the wild, he circled the weakest in the herd and tried to separate her. He needed to isolate his mother to continue his attacks and feed both his anger and his habit. He had loved his father, who deserted him. He loved his sister, who pushed back at him, and he hated his mother because she refused to fight hard enough against him or for his father.

The worse he got, the more Sylvia's once happy life was gone, replaced by a struggle for survival. Caridad moved from listlessness and defenselessness to a mean-spirited resentment aimed at Sylvia. Caridad projected her lost hope onto her daughter. She did everything to make Sylvia's life miserable. She too tried to bully Sylvia, while Ramon remained a miserable, angry presence when home. Sylvia battled her brother constantly and tolerated her mother all in an effort to get through each day. She knew she wanted better, and yet, she could not see it in the present.

With Manuel's visits becoming less frequent and Ramon's thievery becoming more so, there was little, if any, money at home. Regular meals were capricious at best. Caridad would order Sylvia to visit a girlfriend's house, usually Inez, around the dinner hour almost in the hope that her daughter might be invited to stay and eat. Sylvia eventually got an after-school job at the local five-and-dime to pay for her own needs and maybe provide a little extra for her mother. Caridad wanted Sylvia to quit school in order to work full time. Relenting, Sylvia quit school for a time but ended up returning. Sylvia had arrived a bit early to meet her mother at the factory where Caridad worked. When she saw her mother sweating over a sewing machine in a darkened room, back to high school she went.

Sylvia got a job at the movie theater across the street and down the block from her apartment building. It was a full-time position, but while working the night shift, five o'clock in the evening to midnight, so she could attend school. The money was good. Caridad was still very watchful of her daughter, but she was tired too. Sylvia's best friend, Inez, helped lighten the mood outside the apartment and provided Sylvia with any cover she needed to enjoy herself. Sylvia started seeing a boy, Noel, from the neighborhood. He was a year older, which made Caridad a little weary. Over time, she saw he treated her daughter well enough that she began to relent—until she saw him with her son, Ramon, late one night. Caridad was coming back from the market. From the shadows, she saw them together on the corner beneath the streetlight. They were chatting quietly while sharing what appeared to be a cigarette. The pungent smell of the wafting marijuana smoke told Caridad all she needed to know. She slipped quietly past. Back to the apartment, she told Sylvia what she had witnessed and forbade her to see Noel.

Sylvia ignored the order, continuing to see Noel on the sneak. One night while Sylvia was leaving her job at the movie theater, Caridad ran directly at her from across the street; she had suspected correctly that Noel was meeting her daughter. Caridad was waving a very large stick, and she proceeded to beat Sylvia. How dare her seventeen-year-old daughter disobey her mother! Caridad beat her all the way home. Sylvia didn't fight back, as she didn't dare further defy her mother. She was frightened and embarrassed by her mother's public flash of anger. When they got back to the apartment, Caridad went looking for Sylvia's new prom dress and coat—which she had bought with the money from her job at the theater—and using the scissors, she cut them both into tiny pieces. Sylvia was distraught. She knew that she had brought this upon herself with her defiance. Caridad screamed hysterically at her daughter for her deliberate disobedience, reminding her Noel was trouble. He hung around with the wrong people and was probably doing drugs. Sylvia's fear of her mother was stronger than her affection for Noel, and she immediately broke up with him. It turned out for the best. Sylvia would later learn that Noel's path in life would align more with Ramon's than her own.

It took some years, but Sylvia began to see hints of her old mother. They would laugh and share stories and talk about the old days. Sylvia suspected that Caridad now found refuge with Sylvia from the anger she harbored toward her absentee husband and the terror she felt in the presence of her junkie son. Though Caridad was good to Sylvia, at a moment's notice, her mood could change. Ramon didn't help matters much. When he showed up at home, his filthy mouth filled the air with spiteful words. His very presence infected the room with terror. They had both become afraid of Ramon, but Sylvia would never show it.

One night Ramon showed up very high and in a particularly nasty mood. He yelled at Caridad to give him money, which she did not have. He turned his attention to Sylvia, knowing that she worked at the movie theater.

"Syl, give me your money," Ramon demanded.

"No!" Sylvia responded defiantly.

"I swear ... Don't make me ..."

Ramon leapt at Sylvia and tackled her to the ground. They wrestled violently. They rolled around on the floor grappling and knocking over furniture. Once Ramon realized that Sylvia was not going to surrender, he reared back and threw a punch at her, knocking a tooth loose and splattering blood across her blouse. Stunned by the impact, Sylvia lay on the floor holding her mouth and moaning. Ramon seemed stunned as well, more by the shame of striking his sister than the aftermath. He quickly got up and left the apartment, closing the door softly behind him.

While Sylvia's night job paid for her necessities and an occasional small luxury, here it could not pay for major dental repair. A young girl missing a front tooth was not a good cover look. It did not bode well for her current and future employment. She knew her mother didn't have the money. In desperation, she sat down and wrote a letter to her father in Puerto Rico, addressing it to him at the hotel, asking him for the money for her tooth.

Papi,

I haven't asked you for anything all these years, and I don't want anything from you ever. I just need some money to replace a front tooth that fell out of my mouth in an accident. Please send as soon as you can.

Sylvia

It was the first time Sylvia had reached out to her father. She didn't have time for emotions or explanations. She was direct and straight to the point. Diego sent her the money for her dental work.

After this incident, Sylvia came to realize what she probably knew all along. She was pretty much on her own. Her father had left, her brother was lost, and her mother had finally started to assuage her resentment by going out on the town with her old crowd. Caridad had promised Sylvia that when she turned eighteen, she would allow her more freedom as a grown woman. True to her word, Caridad never barked at her daughter when she went out with friends to the movies and dances once she turned eighteen. They started to grow closer to one another.

It was slightly depressing at home, especially when Ramon was around. Sylvia and Caridad were trying to make it more bearable. They cooked and sewed together. They listened to music and danced together. They shared stories about their respective friends. It was only when Ramon was around that the mood was tense and the misery palpable. They had learned to take special care to hide any money or valuables they each had.

SYLVIA, 1953

Sylvia graduated from high school shortly after turning eighteen. She was very proud that she was able to stay the course. Caridad was equally impressed. Sylvia was her only child to complete her education.

Sylvia thought of herself as a woman now. She had become an expert at shielding herself from the ugliness that sometimes lurked in her home. She had a high school diploma. She was somebody! She ventured into Manhattan to get a real job. Caridad was happy but nervous for her daughter. She cautioned her about what awaited beyond the safety of their neighborhood.

"Sylvia, hija, you may encounter a lot of problems when you look for a job."

"Why?"

"La gente no contrata puertorriqueños o negros." Caridad warned her daughter that people don't normally hire Puerto Ricans or people with dark skin.

"Si? But I graduated from high school," Sylvia reminded her mom. "And I have experience working."

"I just wanted to warn you so you won't get your feelings hurt."

"Mommy, I have my diploma, and I'm as good as anyone else. I work hard!"

With that determination, Sylvia put on her best outfit, fashioned by her mother's deft hands, and headed out on her job search. Responding to a want ad in the paper, Sylvia made her way down to Bankers Trust Company on Wall Street. They wanted someone who understood responsibility, had a work ethic, and, although this was not said aloud, was altogether confident and attractive. Sylvia was hired immediately.

Caridad was proud of her daughter. She was educated and working in an office downtown. Sylvia was important now. She worked very hard through the years, climbing out of the typing pool to become a secretary and later supervise the administrators in the legal department. After a long subway ride back to the Bronx, she came home to meals her mother cooked especially for her. She was going out with friends on the weekends to the beach, amusement parks, and dances. Sylvia and Inez assembled quite a cross section of friends, both boys and girls. They were having too much fun to worry about boyfriends.

Life was good. Both Sylvia and her mother worked and came home to have meals together. Ramon had moved farther and farther away from them, visiting only occasional. Sylvia had become an expert at hiding money from Ramon. She hid it in ceiling tiles, under heavy nightstands, and sewn into the inside of her dresses. There was more to hide now. Her friends were starting to marry and settle down, even Inez. Sylvia lost her partner in crime.

When she was twenty, Sylvia reluctantly went with Inez and her husband to a dance at the Hunts Point Palace. The place was crowded with women eager to meet the young men just back from the service. Across the way, Sylvia saw a familiar face that she couldn't quite place. It was a face from Spanish Harlem—a boy who lived around the block from her folks. He was someone she thought both she and Ramon used to see at the candy store before they moved to the Bronx.

"Sylvia?"

"Jhonny, is that you?" Sylvia inquired, pulling his name from her memory.

"Yes. I thought that was you. Wow, it's been a long time. You guys moved to the Bronx, right?"

"Si. Prospect Avenue. And you? Where have you been?"

"My family moved to the Bronx also a few years after yours, but over on Faile Street. I just got out of the army."

Sylvia and Jhonny Quintana caught up quickly. He was a gentleman and came from a good family. Sylvia gave him her phone number, and a courtship began. They enjoyed the movies, dances, and house parties together. Jhonny was easy to be with, kind, and respectful to her in every way. His family— mother, father, and two brothers—lived together in a large apartment. They were the kind of family Sylvia remembered having when she was younger. There was no bitterness or anger in their house, just love and a warm sense of hope.

Sylvia saw in Jhonny a very caring soul, someone whose work ethic, gentleness, and optimistic disposition was a godsend for after all she had suffered at home. Jhonny had a calming, peaceful effect on her. She felt valued and safe. Jhonny also had a car. Girls from her neighborhood didn't typically meet, never mind go out with boys with cars. But the car and Jhonny's age—two years older—caused trouble at home. Caridad tried to prohibit Sylvia from dating Jhonny.

"Mami, I'm twenty years old, a high school graduate making my own money, and very capable of making my own decisions!" Sylvia pleaded.

"Mija ..." Caridad started to respond, but she found it difficult to counter her daughter's logic and eventually relaxed her stance, especially after having met Jhonny several times.

"Esta bien." She finally relented.

Sylvia and Jhonny dated exclusively for two years. It became clear that they both wanted the same things.

They were engaged in April, the Saturday before Easter in 1957. Caridad was very happy for Sylvia. The wedding was planned for the following October. As the time drew nearer to the event, the reality of Sylvia leaving home to start her own family seemed to upset Caridad. It wasn't that she couldn't see the joy of Sylvia and Jhonny; it was that she couldn't escape the feeling of being abandoned, being left behind to deal with the storm that was Ramon. Sylvia was her light. Without her, there would be impenetrable darkness. Caridad couldn't shoulder this burden alone.

Things at home became tense. Sylvia was confused by her mother's sullenness. Ramon's episodic chaos didn't help any. There was a lot of fighting, a lot of crying, and a lot of unpleasantness. Sylvia was embarrassed by it all. She put up a good front. She never told Jhonny about any of this. She kept him away from her apartment, and on the occasions she couldn't, she timed it so that both Ramon and Caridad were out.

Sylvia planned the wedding. Gripped by resentment, her mother would not help. Ramon was high most of the time and oblivious to Sylvia's life, sometimes purposely making things difficult. Sylvia felt anxious. She tried to ignore the pall that hung over her and forged ahead, all while trying to keep Jhonny from her truth at home.

She painstakingly planned her wedding. Ignoring the chaos swirling around her, Sylvia worked on all the details of the big day. Money was tight in that she and Jhonny were paying for this on their own. Neither family was in a position to contribute to the affair. They budgeted paycheck to paycheck to save for the celebration. Sylvia didn't want a huge affair but felt she deserved a wedding with all the trimmings they could afford.

Sylvia had arranged for the photographers to memorialize their day, but she hadn't realized that part of the package included them arriving at her apartment for pictures of the bride preparing on the day of the wedding. Sylvia looked around and realized the apartment, after years of serving as a battleground, was tired and worn. She had one week to clean up the mess.

She started by painting the place. Jhonny didn't help because Sylvia never told him what was going on. Caridad and Ramon just sat around and watched. They sneered defiantly as Sylvia moved and rearranged furniture on her own. She had to work around them from the moment she came home until she collapsed in her bed in the wee hours of the morning. Sylvia got the sense that they were hoping she'd get discouraged and call off the wedding so that she could live with them forever ... in misery. Instead, their obstinance made her even more determined. She was on a mission to redecorate the apartment, and at four o'clock in the morning the day of her wedding, she finished.

Jhonny's parents were very helpful. While they couldn't contribute financially, they offered to help in many ways. His mother said she'd cook for the wedding and told Sylvia about a good friend who could do the flowers. His brothers ran errands for the couple leading up to the big day. This was the kind of support Sylvia longed for from her own family. Jhonny's family volunteered. Jhonny's parents went so far as to invite Sylvia's family over for dinner a couple of weeks before the wedding. She was unsure of how her mother would behave at dinner. She asked Jackie and his wife, Maria, to join them as reinforcements and a buffer. She never mentioned it to Ramon. He would only see it as an opportunity to pillage the apartment.

Caridad was gracious at dinner. It was as though she knew Sylvia needed her to put on the performance of a lifetime. She looked beautiful in a dress she made especially for the occasion, and her manners were impeccable. You could see that Jhonny's parents were captivated. Jackie and Maria were surprised by Caridad's charm.

Finally, the big day arrived. It was a beautiful, bright sunny October day straight from heaven. Caridad had left the apartment earlier and had not returned when Inez, Sylvia's maid of honor, and the other bridesmaids arrived to help her dress. Sylvia was worried that her mother had left in protest and perhaps was not coming back. And Ramon arrived high and in a particularly nasty mood. He did what he could to make things miserable for everyone.

Inez, sensing Sylvia's anguish, whispered quietly in her ear.

"Don't worry about a thing. This is your day. Don't let anything or anyone take that away. I will take care of this. You relax and be the bride!"

Inez subsequently sidled up to Ramon and firmly whispered in his ear.

"Cabron, if you don't quit this shit right now, there's going to be trouble. Your sister means a lot to me, and this is her special day. Entiende?"

She punctuated her point by slowly stepping back and giving Ramon the side-eye stare. Ramon was quiet for a second. He looked at his sister and nodded his head a couple of times in what seemed to be a gesture of understanding. Caridad had returned to the apartment dutifully and stood next to Sylvia in solidarity.

Ramon looked at his mother and then slowly walked over to Sylvia and kissed her on the cheek.

"Hermana, all the best. Te quiero." Then he turned and left the apartment.

That was the last time Sylvia saw Ramon alive.

Jhonny and Sylvia's wedding was quite the affair. After pictures were taken with her mother, they headed off to the church. The ceremony was brief and beautiful. Caridad and Jhonny's parents beamed with pride from the front pew. More photos were taken outside the church, but the wedding party was eager to make their way to a basement near Hunts Point that served as a social club most nights. It was where Jhonny and Sylvia and their friends danced and drank the night away to the sounds of Joe Cuba, an up-and-coming Latin band leader. Joe was a friend of Jhonny's from Spanish Harlem. They grew up playing stickball and hanging at Joe's father's candy store together—which was where Jhonny and Sylvia met as kids. It was a magical night.

Sylvia slipped out the front door for some air. Inez was outside smoking a cigarette. Sylvia dropped into Inez's arms and started to cry.

"What's wrong?" Inez asked her friend.

"Nothing. I'm just so happy," Sylvia explained.

"Ah, that's right. Everything's looking up."

Sylvia picked her head up off Inez's shoulder and nodded in acknowledgement, her eyes still wet with tears.

"My mother behaved," she started. "My brother seemed almost human for a minute, and most of all, I have a new family with Jhonny."

Sylvia drew a big sigh, and her shoulders actually slumped. "I feel like a heavy shadow is gone."

She cried harder, her shoulders shaking.

"I feel … *como se dice?* Relieved? Is that OK?" Sylvia asked, almost seeking forgiveness from Inez for her thoughts.

"Esta bien, mi amiga. Esta bien," Inez reassured her friend while stroking and patting her hand.

EDDY AND RAPPY

"Perdona me." Eddy held out his hand to Gordo in apology. He had to interrupt the narrative to attend to the phone buzzing in his pocket.

"Hey."

"Eddy, it's me, Rappy!"

"Yeah, I know. Remembered your number from last night's conversation. What's up?" Eddy asked.

"It may not be anything, but there's been a whole bunch of chatter going down in the neighborhood."

"What about?"

"Seems that Willy 'Cat Eyes' has disappeared."

"Disappeared?"

"Yeah. He got out of Rikers just a little while ago, and he was laying low—distancing himself from his crew, the Satanic Saints, and trying to stay out of trouble, being on parole and all," Rappy explained.

"And?"

"Well, his girl had their baby and headed way upstate to get away from the life. Everyone assumed that he went to play baby daddy, but when his boys reached out to her, she said he was not with her."

"Yeah, but she could have been playing dumb so that Willy could escape the life."

"That's the thing. I heard Willy's crew was a little suspicious. They kind of got the vibe that he was setting up to pack up and leave, so they sent a few lieutenants to visit the girl, Selena, on the sly—see if they could catch them together."

"Let me guess. They came up empty."

"Yep. Word has it that they set up for a few days, and they saw Selena and the kid but no Willy."

"Um, interesting," Eddy said.

"Yeah, and when they reached out to her again after the visit to see about Willy, she seemed upset. Fact is, she started yelling at them to tell her what they did with Willy," Rappy added.

"Maybe Willy had other plans—other baby mamas."

"Or, if we're playing this guessing game about the DDs, you figure Willy 'Cat Eyes,' the titular head of the Satanic Saints, boyfriend of Selena Valdez, side action for the late Timoteo, may have come up in Tomas's black ops intelligence gathering."

"El le mate." (He killed him.) Eddy finished Rappy's thoughts. "He's evening the score."

"Bingo! And apparently, Willy's number two may have drawn a similar conclusion and is none too happy."

Eddy hung up abruptly, thought to himself for a second, and turned to Gordo. By this time, they had been through a couple of drinks and a few slices of pizza.

"What was that about?" intoned Gordo.

"Another piece to the puzzle. I'll catch you up on it later—once I can pull it all together." Eddy then responded with a thought of his own. "Your mom really had to fight to get to where she is—I mean, where you guys are today."

Gordo nodded his head emphatically.

"Absolutely!"

"Her brother Ramon ... That was painful for her?"

"Yes, she told me they were inseparable as kids, and then the drugs. She said it was truly a case of Dr. Jekyll and Mr. Hyde, and the drugs devoured the good, leaving only the evil behind."

"Ramon died an addict, si?"

"Yes. My mom hadn't seen him in years. She kind of erased him from her life, preferring to remember the good Ramon. Then she got a call one day telling her that her brother was found dead with a needle in his arm in the basement of an apartment that was set on fire in the South Bronx."

"Damn!" Eddy exclaimed.

"Yeah." Gordo continued. "Mom said it was like grieving for someone twice. The first was a loss of a brother, and the second was the loss of a life."

"Do you think your mom's difficult childhood guided her adulthood? I mean, I don't know what I mean. I'm just trying to get a fix on what made your moms tick—what drove her to act."

"My mom was driven. My pops was great, but Mom's struggles were greater coming up. It drove her, and she drove the family bus."

SYLVIA AND JHONNY, 1959

Sylvia and Jhonny worked hard at creating a home together. They moved into a small apartment in the basement of a building on Bryant Avenue in the South Bronx. It was all their own, and they set about decorating it in the most modern way—but within the budget of Sylvia's job at the bank and Jhonny's car mechanic salary. So while it was tasteful, it wasn't extravagant. Sylvia studied the latest home magazines, and like her mother did with clothing, she copied the feel and composition of the latest styles and executed them in her home with whatever was modestly available at the secondhand or bargain stores. Sylvia was intent on continuing her metamorphosis to be a fully integrated American family. While she lived among her own—Inez and her husband lived around the corner, Jackie and Maria lived a few blocks away, and Jhonny's parents were in the vicinity as well—Sylvia was determined that she and Jhonny would blaze a different path: a home in the suburbs, the best and highest education for their kids, and the freedom to enjoy the fruits of a working-class family in America. Jhonny was not the driving force behind this journey. Sylvia had a plan—not detailed maybe but a directional progression that moved deliberately forward.

First up was a family. Sylvia and Jhonny had their first son, Jamie, two years into their marriage. Their next child, Sofia ("like Sofia Loren," Sylvia told anyone who asked), was born a year later, and their youngest, Charlton (yes, after the actor Charlton Heston), another two years after that. Sylvia left the workforce when she started having children. On an as-needed basis, Jhonny waited tables on the weekends to make up the shortfall—as-needed, like when they needed to save for a home. Remembering her cousins who bought their own home when she was younger, Sylvia wanted that independence. She and Jhonny never bought the latest and greatest things, like a color television or stereo, in order to save for the bigger things. Sylvia didn't see this as a struggle but rather as a sacrifice for the greater good.

She wanted her children to enjoy a happy childhood but knew they needed to prepare for tomorrow. They were expected to work hard in school, do their homework, and bring home good grades—no exceptions. Every morning Sylvia would wake the children early to get them ready for school. They would be clean and neat so that everyone knew they were cared for and loved. While they ate their English muffins and sipped their hot chocolate huddled around the open oven for warmth, they were quizzed on their assignments, current events, or cultural milestones. She wanted to send them off with confidence with the answers to the test in school—and life! While she nurtured their intellectual curiosity and encouraged their acceptance of others, she taught the kids to stand up for themselves. She knew that life could be a tough journey.

Jamie entered kindergarten easily. His mother walked him to school a few blocks from their apartment, holding his hand and hoping things would go smoothly. He was a bright child, open to learning and doing new things. He took fairly quickly to the twist, which Sylvia taught him accompanied by The Beatles' "Twist and Shout" at a birthday party. He was quite the little athlete. Jhonny's brothers liked to show him off to their friends. He hit a Spalding pink ball with a sawed-off broomstick pretty far for a five-year-old. He enjoyed reading, preferring it to watching television, but he'd been a bit sheltered under the watchful eye of his family and their extended family in the neighborhood and was very comfortable with the familiar faces. Sylvia wondered how he would do with a new crowd of both kids and adults. As soon as they reached the entrance to his new classroom, Jamie squeezed his mother's hand tightly, smiled up at her, broke from her grip, and then rushed into the room with a laugh toward the gaggle of kids. Sylvia knew he would be fine.

Jamie came home from school one day with his left knee skinned and his shirt slightly torn on the sleeve. Sylvia was shocked when he walked through the door.

"What happened?" she asked.

Jamie started to cry and rushed to his mother's arms while murmuring.

"Some kid pushed me on the playground. He wasn't very nice."

"Why did he do that?"

"I don't know. He's a mean kid. No one likes him."

"Why did he pick on you?"

"I was playing kickball with a bunch of the kids, and he wanted the ball. We told him to wait." Jamie couldn't finish because he slowly started to sob.

"Hijo, look at me. That child is a bully. He pushed you because he wanted to frighten you."

"He scares everyone, Mom."

"Tomorrow, if he pushes you or anyone else, I want you to punch him right in the face. Entiende?"

"Mom! I can't do that—"

"Well, hijo, if you don't do that, you better not come home crying to me, because then I will give you something to *really* cry about!"

Jamie studied his mother to see how serious she was in her guidance. Clearly, she meant business. In order to get Jamie to understand the importance of her instruction, Sylvia told her son a story from her own upbringing.

Sylvia told Jamie that she attended Morris High School, which was a pretty rough-and-tumble school. She was coming down a stairwell by herself one day on her way to another class when she ran into a gang of tough girls a grade above her own. Sylvia was Puerto Rican, and these girls were not. There was not a lot of mixing beyond your own people back then. The leader, Ursel, asked Sylvia her name, but Sylvia didn't stand still while answering. Ursel stopped Sylvia by pointing at the decorative barrette she had in her hair and told Sylvia that she wanted the barrette. The menacing faces and sly smiles behind Ursel punctuated the seriousness of the request.

She explained to Jamie that she realized that if she gave Ursel her barrette, there would be no going back to normal. Ursel and her gang would bully Sylvia whenever they had a chance. Either that, or Sylvia would have to avoid them forever. Having made this calculation, Sylvia said she told Ursel that if she wanted it, she would have to take it from her. Ursel smiled, turned back to her gang, and then lurched forward toward Sylvia. Sylvia, somewhat experienced from her squabbles with Ramon, went into full attack mode. They wrestled, scratched, bit, and slapped each other for what seemed like an hour. There was cheering and jeering from the chorus of gang chicks, but Sylvia did not back down. She gave as good as she got. There was ripped clothing, pulled hair, and enough blood on both of the combatants to suggest that neither was going to yield to the other. Finally, exhausted on the floor in opposite corners, Sylvia and Ursel stared at one another, both breathing deeply and holding back tears. The barrette was on the floor between them. Ursel got up and signaled to her gang with a nod of her head, and they left the stairwell. Sylvia gathered herself, picked up her barrette, and went home to cry on her own.

Jamie was stunned. Sylvia patted his head and finished the tale.

Sylvia said one week later she saw Ursel coming toward her and Inez on the street outside their high school with her gang dutifully in tow. Sylvia's instinct was to cross the street to avoid the confrontation. She did not want to get the shit kicked out of her again, but then she heard Ursel call her name.

"Sylvia, Sylvia!"

Sylvia looked up somewhat surprised and didn't reply at first.

Then she heard Ursel again.

"How are you, girl?"

Before Sylvia could answer, Ursel declared to her minions, "Y'all remember Sylvia? She is one badass bitch! I wouldn't fuck with her. Nah!"

Just like that, Ursel and her mob passed. Ursel gave Sylvia the nod of approval and moved on. Inez asked her how she knew Ursel.

The next day while standing in line for lunch, the bully bumped into Jamie quite by accident. Jamie turned around and punched the kid square in the nose. There was a small crunching sound and blood everywhere. Jamie ended up in the principal's office, and Sylvia was summoned to pick him up. She listened intently to the principal talk to her about her son's need for self-control and discipline. She sat silently and took in the semi-lecture, showing signs of attentiveness to the school official. She grabbed Jamie by the back of his neck and forcefully guided him out of the office and, ultimately, the school. When they were alone walking side by side together, Sylvia looked down at Jamie, who looked slowly back at her. She winked, patted his head, kissed its crown, and smiled. Sylvia didn't like bullies, and she always opted to do what she viewed was right, even if it meant settling it in a fight.

EDDY AND MEL RUBIN

Eddy's phone came to life once more. He dismissed the call and asked Gordo to continue, but the phone buzzed again and again, demanding to be answered.

"Sorry, bro. Let me grab this ... Cepeda."

Once the caller announced himself, Eddy turned his back slightly on Gordo.

"Retired Special Agent Cepeda, this is retired Special Agent Rubin. You called?"

"Yes, thank you for getting back to me so quickly," Eddy responded. "I don't know how to say this, so I'll just say it. A mutual friend from the bureau said you might be able to assist me. It involves an old case of yours and a friend of mine."

"Yes, our friend called me and told me to expect your call. She was insistent that I speak with you. Normally, I wouldn't discuss old cases, especially sensitive ones, but I owe our mutual friend a very large debt that she decided to cash in on your behalf. You must be one of the good guys."

Eddy silently congratulated himself on always working his network and doing for others in order to bank goodwill. His efforts with his former partner were just made money good.

"The names on this case ... Let's just say, this is one of those cases that stays with you a long time—like forever. I think about this one every day, especially recently, which is why I think you're asking around."

Eddy sat up straight.

"Mr. Rubin—may I call you that?"

"No, please call me Mel."

"Mel, can I reach you at this number a little later? I'm in the middle of something right now, but I really would like to talk with you at length."

"Absolutely! By the way, I expected this call about this case," Mel Rubin noted. "I guess I'm just surprised that it came from you—a little far from southern Florida and Texas. This is not exactly your beat, correct?"

Eddy was impressed but not surprised that retired Special Agent Rubin had done a little background check on him.

"Yes, but maybe I'm the only one who ..." Eddy didn't want to finish his thought out loud and in public.

Mel Rubin picked up on Eddy's reticence and gave Eddy an out.

"Cepeda, you have my number, and I have yours. Call me."

"Thank you."

Mel Rubin cut the call before Eddy had the time to get in these last words of appreciation.

"Sorry, Gordo. Your moms was quite a strong woman. Now tell me what you know about your uncle Jackie."

JACKIE, BORN 1930

Joaquin, "Jackie" to most, Sylvia's older brother and Caridad and Diego's firstborn, practically raised himself. His parents were busy making a life born of toils in the kitchen of the Plaza Hotel and the dress factory downtown, not that he felt denied of any love or affection. Jackie was just born older. In the familiar confines of Spanish Harlem and then the Bronx, Jackie wandered around among his cousins and the other neighborhood kids. Unlike his youngest siblings, he didn't find a bond within the family ties. While well fed, sheltered, and taken care of by his parents and his extended family, Jackie was born a child of the streets. He found affinity among his peers. He was especially tight with the Montenegro kids, who lived on their block in Spanish Harlem.

Jackie and Maria Montenegro, the oldest daughter of the clan, were invariably in each other's classes at school. Along with the other public school kids, they attended catechism with one another, learning to be good Catholic children for their Holy Communion and, ultimately, their confirmation. They teased one another incessantly.

"Tu eres fea" Jackie would tell Maria how ugly she was. She wasn't.

"Biente por carajo!" Maria would tell Jackie to go fuck himself.

Yet, despite this combative banter, they were sweet on each other. Jackie noticed her immediately when they met in grammar school. Her doe eyes, perfectly symmetrical face, heart-shaped chin, and the jet black braided hair just got him all hectic inside. Maria was taken by him as well but in a different way. It was not so much the way he looked. She was just amazed at his size. He was so much bigger than their other classmates—not taller, just thicker with a large patch of wavy brown hair. She did not think of Jackie as fat, just outsized. While he overshadowed others with his physical presence, it was his gentility that Maria found attractive. She was intrigued by this combination of size and sincerity. From the very beginning, there was this odd bond between them. They were very protective of one another. Jackie spent much of his time over at the Montenegro apartment

Inevitably, Jackie befriended the twins, first Paolo and Pablo and then Tomas and Timoteo. Jackie became an extension of their family. To the youngest Montenegro sister, Elenita, he was like another older brother. Eventually, Jackie became an outside member of the roaming Montenegro Doble Doble pack. He was not all with them, as his parents moved to the Bronx when he was eleven and kept him busy most weekends with their excursions to the beaches and the parks, but he was someone the boys felt they knew well and trusted. As much as he could, often cutting school, he ventured back and forth to Manhattan via the subway to see Maria and her brothers. When Maria became pregnant, the Montenegros were not angry or disappointed; rather, they were thrilled to have Jackie marry into the family.

Having their first, Juan Carlos, whom they called JC, was cause for celebration. Despite the fact that these kids—Jackie was nineteen and Maria, eighteen—were having kids of their own, the Cruz and Montenegro families welcomed this child into their world. Jackie and Maria waited almost ten years before having other children, but soon thereafter, they had three other kids, all girls. They settled in the South Bronx, not far from Sylvia and Caridad.

JC, like his father, was well taken care of by his immediate and extended family, but he was also a child of the streets. The late fifties and early sixties were an especially perilous time in the dark recesses of New York City. There were far too many bad guys, distractions, and pitfalls lurking beyond the cozy confines of the family's imagined boundaries, and JC was an explorer.

Tomas Montenegro was very protective of his sisters, especially the eldest, Maria. He liked Jackie very much and took a special interest in him for the sake of the family. As such, the Montenegro boys set Jackie up at Hunts Point Junk & Salvage, where he started in the yard and worked his way up to supervisor over time. The work was hard and dirty but honest. He made a good living, enough for him and Maria to put some money aside for a rainy day. One day Tomas came by the shop and asked for Jackie. Jackie greeted his brother-in-law in the office with a quick hug and kiss on the cheek. They exchanged pleasantries, inquiring about each other's family while having a few laughs to fill the gaps in conversation. Tomas told Jackie he had a sensitive piece of business that needed to be handled delicately in the yard.

"Jackie, we got a couple of cars"—he hesitated before proceeding— "that I need to have disassembled in the evenings here in the yard."

"Disassembled?" Jackie inquired

"Yeah, we think they're worth more for their parts than they are whole. Entiende?"

"Sure." Jackie was starting to get the gist.

Hunts Point Junk & Salvage had always been a legitimate business, owned in part by the Montenegros but always on the up and up. Jackie sensed that this was about to change. Tomas was suggesting chop shop–like activities.

"Any problems, Jackie?"

"Nah. When you say the evenings, what do you mean?"

"After you close for business."

"I just would have to tell Maria that I'm working late a couple of nights, but this shouldn't be a problem."

Tomas held his hand up, palm out toward Jackie, suggesting that he slow down.

"I need the yard, I don't need you. I will bring in my own crew of guys. You go home to my sister."

"But—" Jackie started

"No buts," Tomas insisted. "We don't want you involved. Just want to let you know so you can get your people out at the end of the day. Don't need anyone putting in overtime."

"Tomas, I'd be happy—"

"I know you would. Don't worry. We'll give you a little something for ... shall we say, keeping your people on the clock and out by closing."

Tomas moved to Jackie, cupped his hand around his brother-in-law's neck, pulled him closer, and kissed the top of his head.

This is how it all started.

Jackie was never directly involved in any criminal activities, and he was only tangentially associated with the Doble Doble. The brothers were careful to give their sister's husband plausible deniability—a legal term they learned from their lawyers. They asked him for favors and had him run errands. They never ordered Jackie to do anything. It was always presented as a favor. They never shared details of their operations or activities, and Jackie never asked. The brothers would call from time to time with some seemingly innocuous jobs: drive and deliver a package to a friend or associate, drop off an envelope at a storefront, make a call to inquire about the hours a business might be open—all necessary steps in larger intricate plans but ones that didn't need any firepower, muscle, or intellect. Jackie was a useful body to the Doble Doble. He allowed their crew to use their talents in more productive areas. And the brothers paid Jackie and, by extension Maria, exorbitantly for pedestrian tasks. The family was taking care, and being careful, with its own. Jackie had his day job but made a little on the side by helping his brothers-in-law with some minor favors.

Jackie and Maria always liked going to City Island in the summer. Jackie had great memories of his own family going there right before his pops split. This little island in the Bronx, at the extreme western end of Long Island Sound, was a small oasis for the borough's inhabitants. The long, narrow road heading to the docks was lined on either side with seafood restaurants and little shops specializing in all that makes a summer night—fried clams, cotton candy, ice cream, T-shirts, and novelties. Jackie enjoyed eating at the picnic tables near the docks and watching the boats coming in and out of their slips. He eavesdropped on the local fishermen lying to one another about the size of their catches, as well as the locals bargaining for their share of fish.

Jackie was known to come here on the weekends with one or two of his kids in tow to drop a line in the water off the dock. The languid pace of the afternoon suited him as he sat and smoked his cigarettes, drank a few beers, and was lulled by the water lapping rhythmically against the wooden pylons. He loved the smell of the breeze off the water. He dreamed of fishing off his own boat one day. With the money he was putting aside for helping his brothers-in-law, it might be possible.

EDDY AND GORDO AT MANNY'S

"Dos mas, por favor!" Eddy, pulling away from the conversation for a second, waved down the waiter and asked for two more drinks, Corona and lime for Gordo and another Cuba libre for himself.

"So your uncle was pretty content, no? The Montenegros took care of him. He had his own family, a job, and a little money on the side. Yes?"

"Yes," Gordo agreed. "But then the thing with JC changed everything."

JC, BORN 1949

JC was born in 1949. A child born to children, he was loved, adored, and spoiled by his parents, their parents, and the entire neighborhood. For Maria and Jackie, parenting him was on-the-job training. JC was a restless baby, needing and screaming for constant attention. He was also very active. He once climbed out of his crib and broke his little leg from the fall. It was quite a sight to see a toddler in a tiny cast. Uncomfortable and feeling restricted in his movements, JC soon figured out how to slip out of his cast. Jackie and Maria had their work cut out for them. They often fell asleep seated at the foot of JC's crib in their living room, their heads resting against each other, exhausted from chasing him all day and then singing songs to coax him to slumber.

He grew up in the age of Aquarius—hippies, counterculture, and drugs. A whole new generation was experiencing puberty during the advent of the Vietnam War. This first wave of the baby boomers was teeming with energy, curiosity, and disregard for authority. It wasn't that they were disrespectful; it was that they actively questioned established ways and what they viewed as conventional. The outgrowth of this movement was the emergence of a counterculture where all social norms were resisted. Protest marches, long hair, burning bras, and sexual freedom assaulted tradition on all fronts. JC tried to fit in among his family and did his best to hang within this tight circle, but he was extremely curious. Unlike many of his friends, JC wasn't an athlete. He tried the usual games—stickball, two-hand touch, even basketball, which at his height (he was more than six feet by the time was fifteen) would have been natural—but nothing stuck with him. Music, on the other hand, really called to him. He found it intriguing and seductive.

Santos, his grandmother's youngest brother, was a musician. He played the piano and various percussion instruments—specializing in the conga drums—for house bands at clubs in Harlem and occasionally the Village. JC adored and respected his father, but he always thought Santos was one cool cat. Santos wore porkpie hats and suspenders that draped over his reedlike body and smoked clove cigarettes. Santos practiced his beats most afternoons on the stoop of his apartment building down the block from JC. He drew a small audience to these impromptu concerts, but none so enthralled as JC. Santos enjoyed talking to his young admirer. They spent hours discussing the evolution of musical genres and musicians from blues to jazz, Mongo Santamaria to Herb Alpert, but JC was especially consumed with hearing Santos's tales of the evolution Afro-Latino music.

Santos enjoyed telling JC that everyone knows that slaves were brought from Africa to America—especially to work the fields and plantations of the South—in the early days of this nation's founding. However, few recalled that many, many years before these events a majority of the slaves were brought from Africa to Latin America and the Caribbean as agricultural, menial, domestic, and mining workers for the colonists who conquered these lands. In fact, during this time, Santos would state as fact that nine out of ten slaves ended up in Latin America with the balance going to North America. From these roots, Latinos evolved into an exotic mixture of culture, language, and music. Santos told JC that the slave trade in Latin America influenced the color palate of its people. From white, brown, and black, Latinos were a kaleidoscope of shades of skin tone, hair color, and eye color. Similarly, the music evolved like a giant gumbo spiced with many influences that flavored today's blues, jazz, and salsa. JC could barely contain himself. He was intoxicated by this ancestry—this knowledge. With a friend or two, JC tagged along with Santos to the musical venues downtown. Soon, JC was heading downtown without Santos and sometimes without his friends.

Despite protestations from his parents, JC decided that he'd study music after high school at the New School in New York City's Greenwich Village. While not formally trained, JC spent a great deal of time soaking up lessons from Santos and the other musicians he met during his regular excursions to Harlem and the Village. He had spent many hours literally banging on drums on the stoop of his apartment building. He had become quite accomplished on the drums and with other percussion instruments. His swagger helped the admissions committee imagine the possibilities of the raw talent on display during JC's audition. Certainly, the sight of a very tall brown-skinned Puerto Rican wearing puka beads with oversized hands, a large afro, and a beard seemed to defy the norm for most musical academies, but the New School was quite progressive. JC was accepted, and as a mere teenager, he soon moved to the Village.

What Santos excluded, or rather soft-pedaled, from their many talks about the music scene was the underbelly of drug use among the community of musicians. Louis Armstrong said marijuana was better than whiskey. Miles Davis and Ray Charles fought heroin addictions. Not confined to only the brightest stars, drugs permeated even the most pedestrian of musicians. The combination of seductive music and the age of Aquarius made drugs more prevalent than any other time before. JC was not immune. Reintroduced to a little Mary Jane by a nimble nymphet from Scarsdale, JC was soon smoking a couple of times a week. He experimented with speed and finally graduated to *h* —heroin.

JAMIE AND SOFIA

Right after their meeting at Manny's, Eddy and Gordo agreed that they had to hunt down some of the scattered pieces of the mosaic, as Eddy called them, to see if there were any discernible patterns that offered them a clue to the theory of a message and an execution. Since receiving Gordo's secret burner phone package in Puerto Rico, Eddy had been very busy on his end. Gordo told Eddy that he had done some initial sleuthing himself with the help of his tech geek of a sister, Sofia. Sofia Loren Quintana was a few years younger than her brother, Gordo—who she preferred to call by his given name, Jamie—but lightyears ahead of him intellectually. She attended the Choate School on scholarship and then entered the honors program at Carnegie Mellon University, graduating summa cum laude. She graduated with a job at IBM where she worked for many years before being recruited away by a Greenwich-based private equity firm to be a tech analyst.

Although Sofia didn't subscribe to her brother's conspiracy theories around their mother's death, she agreed to help him look into a few things. A little bit after the funeral, they both went back to their mother's home to search for clues. While sifting through her desks, closets, and datebooks, the siblings remarked that they felt like the police executing a search warrant. They found the package Jamie had given back to his mother. The note and the hot sauce were missing, but the parcel was as Jamie remembered it—addressed to him, his mother's return address as sender with a postal stamp from her local post office.

Jamie made a mental note to track down where the hot sauce was distributed. Sofia found her mother's credit card statements and decided to go online using the information she'd found to create several online accounts in Sylvia's name. She had her mother's account numbers, Social Security number, date of birth, and, with Jamie's help, the answers to the various security questions like, "Which one of these addresses below did you ever live at?" After a while, Sofia was able to comb through her mother's credit card transactions for the last few years. She found nothing unusual in any of the purchases except for a regular purchase of airline tickets. Sofia was able to track down the destinations of those flights. There was nothing out of the ordinary about air travel, but in the last few years, Sylvia seemed to go every three months to Florida. Prior to that time, some of her regular travel was to Indiana and Puerto Rico. She traveled by herself while her husband, Jhonny (their father), was still alive and continued the practice after he passed.

"Jamie, did Mom ever tell you about her trips to Florida?" Sofia asked.

Jamie considered this before answering.

"I know that when the girls were looking into colleges, she took them on campus visits to Florida," Jamie said, referring to his adopted cousins, Maria Montenegro Cruz's girls.

"Yeah, I remember that too. But the Florida visits I'm seeing on her credit cards were every three months or at least three times a year. One ticket for herself, no one else."

"Hmm. I know she has some relatives in Orlando, and she mentioned every once in a while that she would go visit them. I think ..." he said, his words trailing off.

"That makes sense. I seem to recall that too. Orlando has its own airport, correct? I mean, with all those kids visiting Mickey Mouse and all."

"Yes, of course. A very busy airport, I would imagine."

"Then why would Mom fly only to the Palm Beach or Fort Lauderdale airports?" Sofia questioned.

"That's strange," Jamie agreed. "I think that Orlando is a couple of hours' drive from either spot—not ideal for visiting Orlando."

"And that's the strange thing as well."

"What?"

"Well, if she flew into the airport at Orlando, we might assume her relatives would pick her up and let her stay at their place and maybe cook for her."

"Yeah, so where are you going with all that?"

"Here's the strange thing. She flies into Palm Beach or Fort Lauderdale. There are no transactions for a rental car, a cab, or an Uber. There are no transactions for a hotel and no transactions during any of these trips for restaurants in Florida. Period!"

"What are you getting at?"

"Well, we've already established that Orlando would be the natural place to visit those relatives. Assume she couldn't *ever* get a flight there. So do her cousins pick her up hours away every time? Wouldn't she rent a car from time to time to save them the trouble? During any of her visits, don't you think she'd treat them to a meal out some time?"

"I see what you're getting at. What are the other towns served by Palm Beach and Fort Lauderdale?"

"Let me Google that." Sofia punched in the question into her computer and read the towns aloud.

"For Fort Lauderdale, we have Dania Beach, Hollywood, Sunrise, and Davie. For Palm Beach, Boca Raton, Boynton Beach, Delray Beach, and Jupiter."

"I've heard of those towns, but none of them mean anything to me as it relates to Mom."

"Jamie, I don't think Mom visited relatives in Orlando. I think she went somewhere else, either to one of these towns or somewhere else in south Florida."

"How far is Miami from those airports?" Jamie inquired.

Sofia was already typing the query into Google.

"Anywhere from ninety minutes to a few hours, depending on which airport, time of the day, and traffic."

"Again, she'd need a car. Not that Miami means anything."

"Jamie, let me try something else."

Sofia typed furiously at the computer. She was flying around various sites, always coming back and seemingly checking things against her mother's credit card transactions.

"That's strange," she finally said. "The same pattern occurs on her trips to Indiana and Puerto Rico. While Florida was her quarterly destination most recently, a few years back, Indiana and PR were her preferred destinations. And again, no other transactions after the airport—no rental cars, hotels, or restaurants."

"Strange," said Jamie, truly perplexed by this newly discovered bizarre behavior.

"Jamie, what if she were being met by someone at the airport who lived or worked somewhere in the area, and they wanted to keep these regular meetings secret?"

"Why?"

"I'm more curious about who."

Jamie and Sofia dug deeper. Again using Sofia's technical skills, they were able to access their mother's phone records, both landline and mobile. Nothing! No calls to Florida, to Orlando, or to anywhere else that coincided with her trips. Sofia then traced their mother's geolocator—Jamie didn't know what that was—through her smartphone, sifted through her email traffic, wandered around her social media accounts, and examined any digital footprints their mother had left. Nothing related to her travels, and nothing related to their investigation. Any momentum behind their search ground to a halt.

After lunch, Sofia decided to return to old-school methods. She and Jamie sat around and asked one another questions about where Mom and Dad hid their birthday gifts or Christmas gifts. What did they do to keep the adult stuff away from the kids? Jamie offered that their father hid issues of *Playboy* in his sock draw. There was no sock drawer any longer and certainly no *Playboy* magazines.

Then it hit them both almost simultaneously. Mom and Dad never liked keeping all their money at the bank. Despite her working at a bank when she was younger, Sylvia was always worried about what she heard had happened during the Great Depression when the banks shut down. In addition, Mom had gotten into the habit of hiding things away from her years of fending off Ramon. Dad, working in the restaurants, sometimes came home with a lot of cash. When they thought the kids weren't looking, their parents would lift the very heavy nightstand on Dad's side of the bed and slip an envelope full of money underneath. Mom also liked to hide things in the drop-down ceiling tiles in the bathroom. The kids knew about these places but never said anything, and they never ventured to see what was hidden in these spots.

Jamie and Sofia practically sprinted to the bathroom to check the ceiling tiles. After lifting a few tiles, they found a manila folder stuffed neatly with newspaper articles and other papers. Nothing else was there. They then went to the heavy nightstand that was still in their mother's bedroom. Beneath it they found an envelope stashed with money—a lot of money. There was at least two thousand dollars in the envelope all in twenties and hundred-dollar bills.

Grabbing the file folder, Jamie and Sofia sat down on their mom's bedroom floor—Sofia with her legs folded in and crossed, while Jamie was splayed out, legs everywhere—to carefully study the contents. There were newspaper clippings concerning the Montenegro Doble Doble. The coverage included a brief history and allegations surrounding the family, the FBI investigations, and the brothers' arrests, trials, and subsequent sentencing. They knew that their mom was related by marriage to the Montenegros. There were also prayer cards from two long-ago funerals. One was for their cousin, JC. This card, not surprisingly, was from Ortiz's Funeral Home. The other was for a young woman who died around the same time as JC. It was for Lisa Rubin, and the card was from the Edwin L. Bennett Funeral Home in Scarsdale, New York. They seemed to recall that this was JC's girlfriend in college, and she had died an addict with him. There were also newspaper clippings of each of their obituaries. JC's was fairly short—a quick accounting of his upbringing, surviving relatives, and where he went to college—that appeared in the *New York Daily News* without an accompanying photograph. Lisa Rubin's was rather lengthy—detailing her accomplishments at a fancy and famous music school in Scarsdale, as well as her scholarship to the New School for her vocal talents. It provided the backgrounds of her parents, their lineage, and the details of their lives, paying

111

special attention to her father, Special Agent Mel Rubin of the FBI. All this was printed in the *New York Times*, accompanied by a studio-quality picture of Lisa, obviously from a yearbook. Their mother would have commented to them that even in death there was social stratification.

Sofia quickly got up from her sitting position on the floor and bolted for her mother's computer. She immediately looked at the search box history of her mother's browser and found what she was looking for right there among the many searches over the last few months of her life. There were several iterations of inquiries on Google for "Montenegro Doble Doble" and "Tomas Montenegro." The search history's busiest periods seemed to coincide with what Jamie had told her was Tomas Montenegro's release date from prison. On a whim, Sofia Googled "Mel Rubin, FBI". She didn't find much at first, but combing through troves of records and arcane references on several news association and government websites, Sofia was able to piece together that Special Agent Rubin was somehow involved with the case against the Doble Doble. Although startled at first, she wasn't really surprised. What did surprise her and Jamie tremendously was that Special Agent Mel Rubin was now retired and living in Delray Beach, Florida.

With Eddy's direction, Jamie and Sofia circled back on a couple of things. Sofia called their relatives in Orlando under the guise of wanting to know more about their relation to their mom for the legacy benefit of building a family tree. While the relatives were reminiscing about their childhood with her mom, Sofia coyly asked them when their mother last visited them in Florida. The question was met with a pause as they tried to recall the last time Sylvia had visited. They admitted that it had been at least ten years.

Jamie busied himself with Googling "hot sauce" and looking at the pictures of labels to jog his memory of the brand that was in Jackie's coffin—the same one mailed to his home with a cryptic note supposedly from his mother. He finally found it: Pique de Isle. This particular sauce *of the island* was made in small batches and was known for its extra kick and green color. Unfortunately, it was available all over Puerto Rico with decent distribution throughout the small foodie shops and bodegas that were sprinkled throughout the tristate area in New York and in Florida. It also did a fairly robust online business. When he was alive, Jackie probably picked it up either in the neighborhood or on one of his occasional trips back to Spanish Harlem. This large network of distribution outlets would be daunting to sift through.

Jamie relayed what he learned to Eddy. Eddy knew tracing the hot sauce purchase was a long shot and probably a dead end, but the travel history was more promising. In addition, Sylvia's interest in the Montenegro legal proceedings in and of itself was not unusual, but the prayer card for Lisa Rubin, whose father was FBI, caught his attention, and so did Lisa's obituary. The prayer card suggested that Sylvia may have attended Lisa Rubin's services.

Eddy knew it was time to reach out again to his former partner and cash in another chit. He started to see some semblance of a pattern or at least some order to a bunch of random facts. Sylvia had traveled on a regular basis, by herself, to a few locations, Florida being the most recent and most frequent. Other than the airline ticket purchase, she was careful not to send out a beacon indicating her whereabouts upon arrival—no calls to or within Florida, no transportation from and back to the airport, and no other credit card receipts for restaurants, hotels, or anything. She salted away a fairly large amount of cash and stashed it in secret, but this was not unusual for her. Cash left few traces. Sylvia, an incidental victim of the Montenegro Doble Doble, was particularly interested in the brothers' legal proceedings, their subsequent incarceration, and ultimate release. Was it a casual interest, or did it reflect what she felt they had taken from her? Eddy then added to these series of musings the fact that JC, her nephew, died with his girlfriend, whose father, Mel Rubin, happened to be FBI and later became connected with the Montenegro case. Special Agent Rubin, widowed some time ago, lived in Delray Beach, a community serviced by both the Palm Beach and Fort Lauderdale airports.

EDDY AND MEL

Retired Agents Rubin and Cepeda agreed to meet at Bryant Park in Midtown Manhattan right behind the New York Public Library. It was just after noon, and the business lunch crowd and tourists were swarming the public park. They grabbed one of the round green tables with matching chairs that were scattered throughout the park. They each sipped coffees they had arrived with.

"Mel, thank you for taking the time to meet me."

"Kid, you're lucky I happen to be in New York these last few days. I'm usually in Delray Beach, Florida, most of the year. Better weather, great beaches, and no state taxes."

"Well, I'll take luck like this any time."

"Cepeda, do you know why I'm in New York and why I picked this place in particular to meet?"

"I can guess why you're in New York. It coincides with why I reached out to you, correct?"

"Indeed! I helped put together a case against a certain locally based criminal family operation some years back. It resulted in several arrests and convictions of what we'd deem were high-value targets. And I recently learned that a tangential—no, incidental—member of said family was slain in a robbery gone bad. Am I tracking here?" Mel asked.

"Yes," Eddy confirmed.

"Good. Now let me tell you why I picked this beautiful sanctuary behind the very august New York Public Library."

"Please."

"Back in the seventies, you may recall that this place was not quite as pristine as it is today. In fact, it was infested with much of the underbelly of the city—small-time gamblers, prostitutes, homeless, and drug addicts. It was so bad that both tourists and natives steered clear. They called it Needle Park!"

Mel looked up at Eddy to make sure he was following along, and he continued with his history lesson.

"Here you have this prestigious place in the New York Public Library, and behind it was the city's outhouse. After a couple of the city's upstanding citizens and businessmen got mugged here, there was a real effort to clean up the cesspool and reclaim the park."

Eddy nodded his head, although he didn't know where Mel was going with this particular story.

"As you can see, with some effort, a lot of money, and some important friends, this park was resurrected and saved from the ravages of illicit activities that were destroying it. My case was part of the attempt to clean up the cesspool."

"The Doble Doble," Eddy intoned.

"Yes, and it took the courage of someone who was familiar with the DD filth to set the case in motion and ultimately clean up the mess for a time. The difference between that crusade and the cleaning up of Bryant Park is that it was done with a lot less fanfare, money, and community support—a heroic effort for soldiers of justice."

"And now that person's dead."

Mel took a deep breath in and looked around as though searching for the appropriate words to respond to Eddy's assertion.

"It's not that simple of an answer."

Eddy was puzzled.

Mel continued.

"Agent Cepeda, Sylvia Quintana's death, if, in fact, it was *not* an accident, is tragic on many levels. Call it an execution or a hit by someone looking to settle a perceived score. Whatever you call it, it is a case of mistaken identity. What do people say of such situations? Right church, wrong pew?"

Eddy leaned back suddenly in his chair, a sign that he was reeling from this bit of information, but he was careful not to allow it to register on his face.

"Again, not to pry too much into official business, but Mrs. Q., Sylvia, wasn't your CI?"

"No, not officially. Our main CI was someone who was familiar with the Montenegro Doble Doble, but it wasn't Sylvia Quintana."

"But I thought she ..."

Feeling a little unsure of his next line of inquiry, he just left the unfinished question hang in the air while Mel finished his narrative.

"Again, getting back to my Bryant Park story. Sylvia Quintana and I shared some very painful history together. We were directly impacted by the drug trade in the seventies, and we both suffered personal collateral damage from its cancerous reach—her nephew and my own daughter. So, we met because of this unfortunate set of circumstances. She wanted to clean up the mess, and so did I!"

JC AND SYLVIA, 1969

Sylvia was just fifteen when JC was born, and in a dark world, this little guy would prove to be a light of shining hope. He was a welcome reprieve from the pain and anguish she was experiencing at home after her father left, while aftershocks of her mother and Ramon were still rippling through the ground beneath her. Jackie and Maria were so filled with joy that it was infectious. At the same time, these young parents were frazzled and exhausted, allowing Sylvia to step in from time to time to save the day. On weekend days, Sylvia spent a fair amount of time babysitting JC. She gladly volunteered not only to squeeze his fat cheeks and smell Johnson's baby shampoo in his hair, but it was also a useful excuse to slip out of the apartment. Caridad put on a brave face from time to time to visit her grandson, but the effort was forced and so at odds with the pain that tortured her.

"Titi" Sylvia relished her time with the little guy. She grew close to JC over the years. She taught him to dance, and coaxed Jhonny to try to teach him to play stickball. At the age of eight, JC was a ring bearer in Sylvia and Jhonny's wedding. When he was ten, Maria and Jackie gave JC a sister, which he wasn't exactly thrilled about. However, around the same time, when his "Titi" Sylvia brought around a boy cousin, Jamie, he was ecstatic. Sylvia saw JC taking an interest in her uncle Santos's music. Her uncle Santos was always an odd one with his music, somewhat simple but harmless nonetheless—or so she thought. She was very proud of JC's admission to the New School. Sylvia was happy in her new family with Jhonny and similarly appreciative of how life was unfolding for Jackie and Maria's family.

One night Sylvia received a collect call. JC was on the line and wanted to charge the call to her telephone account.

"Will you accept the charges?" the operator asked.

"Yes," Sylvia spat out, bewildered. "JC, you OK?"

"Titi," JC muttered slightly audible, "I need help."

"Qué pasó mi sobrino?" Sylvia asked.

"I'm in trouble ... and I ... can't get out ... It's that shit that Ramon ..."

Sylvia knew instantly.

"Where are you?" she asked.

"At a payphone outside my apartment near school."

She asked for the address, told him to stay put, and called Inez to watch the kids. She called Jhonny and asked him to meet her at the downtown subway entrance near their apartment.

Sylvia didn't know what to expect when she got down to JC's apartment. She braced for the worst when she knocked on the door. When there was no immediate answer, she tested to see if it was locked. It wasn't. She looked at Jhonny quickly and then pushed the door open slowly and stepped into a dark and dirty apartment. No surface was uncovered. Sylvia found JC on his bed either asleep, passed out, or dead. She watched his chest to see if she could detect it rising and falling, denoting life. He was always tall and thin, but now at twenty, he appeared fragile. His eyes had deep, dark circles beneath them, and when he at

119

last peered up at her, his eyes seemed hollow. She could breathe. He was alive.

With all the energy he could muster, JC smiled slightly at Sylvia. When he turned his gaze to both she and Jhonny, he started to cry.

"Titi, what do I tell my parents?"

"Shush, JC, don't speak right now. Let us get you out of here."

"Is Lisa still here?"

"Who's Lisa?" Sylvia asked, confused.

"My girlfriend ... Is she ..."

Sylvia and Jhonny quickly canvassed the apartment and found a young girl, arms and legs akimbo, lying on the bathroom floor. Sylvia rushed to her side, put her head on the girl's chest, which was covered in vomit, and listened to her shallow breathing.

"Lisa?" Sylvia said softly.

Recognizing her name but not the person who had spoken it, Lisa lifted her head in slow motion and uttered a shaky response.

"Yeah?"

"Lisa, I'm JC's aunt, Sylvia. My husband, Jhonny, and I are going to take him home. Is there someone we can call for you?"

Lisa hesitated at first, and then looking out the door at JC lying on the bed in Jhonny's arms, she mumbled,

"My mom."

After cleaning the young girl up as best she could and steadying her enough to have her to sit on the toilet seat, Sylvia was able to coax a home telephone number out of her. Sylvia told Jhonny to stay in the apartment while she ran out to find the pay phone.

Sylvia dialed the 914 area code in Westchester and in a minute shattered the world of a suburban couple by telling them how she had found their daughter and where they should come to collect her.

Sylvia waited for Lisa's parents. When they arrived, she relayed what she had encountered upon her arrival. Sylvia gave them her telephone number and offered to help in any way she could. Mr. Rubin returned the gesture by offering his business card. Sylvia didn't know if any of this would prove to be helpful, but in her experience, people in distress would grasp at any lifeline of hope they could. It might provide more succor in the moment than any real sustenance long term. What Sylvia didn't know at the time was that Lisa's father, being a special agent in the FBI, viewed all sources of information as valuable until proven otherwise. The Rubins were still processing the shock, but Mel was very appreciative of the call.

After putting Lisa in their car, the Rubins offered their assistance with JC. Sylvia and Jhonny said they'd be fine. When the Rubins departed, Sylvia and Jhonny folded JC's foal-like frame, all legs and arms, between them and carried him out to the sidewalk. Realizing that they couldn't possibly take him uptown on a subway, they hailed a cab.

Sylvia called her brother Jackie to tell him she had JC at her apartment. Jackie was shocked.

"Why didn't he call me or Maria?" he asked.

"Hermano, I don't know, but maybe he's a little embarrassed."

"Embarrassed?!" Jackie yelled into the phone. "Cono! What the fuck?!"

"Jackie, you should come over right now," Sylvia said. "He's in rough shape."

Jackie and Maria rushed over to Sylvia and Jhonny's place. They saw their son curled up in a ball on the bed. Maria sat down next to her boy, stroked his hair, and whispered a blessing to him while asking what happened.

"Ay bendito mi hijo! ¿Qué pasó?"

"La mierda de tus hermanos es lo que pasó."

Having lived this firsthand with Ramon, Sylvia spit out rather quickly that the shit of Maria's brothers was what happened.

Maria was taken back.

"Callate la boca."

Jackie stared at Sylvia and told her to be quiet. Sylvia got up and walked out of the room.

JC was strung out but aware enough to know he was struggling and needed help. Sylvia was not only the fun aunt but also the one person he thought of in his family as being responsible. Sylvia seemed to get things done. Jackie and Maria were good parents but a little less available in their roles. After getting JC back home, Sylvia asked Jackie and Maria what they intended to do to help JC kick his habit. Jackie and Maria seemed at a loss as to what to do next. Sylvia said that they had to do something—and do it quickly. The struggle that JC was having now would be nothing compared to what it would become if they hesitated or, worse yet, did nothing, hoping it would just get better. As she knew all too well, it wouldn't. Jackie and Maria seemed helpless.

Sylvia called her local priest, Father Felipe Lupe—"Father Phil." Sylvia was very active in the church's programs for kids in the neighborhood. She and Jhonny volunteered for food drives and helped out during the annual church bazaar. Father Phil said he did work at Montefiore Hospital in the Bronx and was aware of their programs for addicts. Without being asked, Father Phil volunteered to make a call for JC. Sylvia related the conversation to Jackie and Maria.

"He's not an addict, Sylvia!" Maria responded sharply

"Maria, JC is a good kid who got in a little over his head with these drugs."

"Don't you judge him!" Maria chided Sylvia. "He's under a lot of pressure at school, and he was trying to fit in—that's all. He's not one of these street addicts!"

"Maria, call it what you will, but JC needs help to get off this shit, and he can't do this on his own. You and Jackie can't do it, and neither can I."

Sylvia finished and looked at Jackie for some support. Jackie just stared straight ahead. Maria was as angry as she had ever been. Her face was taut as she clenched her teeth. She was defending her son but also herself. She also always felt that Sylvia thought she was better than her and her family, the Montenegros. Maria wouldn't stand for Sylvia to judge her or her son. She didn't know what to do, so she bluffed and deflected.

"Sylvia, I don't know why JC called you, but we appreciate what you and Jhonny did for JC. Jackie and I can figure it out from here," Maria stated dismissively.

Sylvia's mouth dropped slightly as she stared through Maria stunned by her sister-in-law's naïveté.

"Excuse me for giving a shit, but your son is fucking doing heroin. He's not smoking an occasional joint. He's a fucking user of smack! Call him whatever the fuck you want to, addict or not, but this shit has a hold of him and won't let go! Trust me!"

"Out!" Jackie pointed at the door and yelled.

Sylvia, arched her eyebrows, raised her voice and then unloaded.

"Listen to me. JC may not be my son, but I love that boy. I love you both as well, but this is not something you can just decide on later. He needs help *ahora*! Now!"

"Let me call my brothers," Maria responded

Sylvia tried to contain her anger by folding her arms tightly across her chest and pursing her lips, but she just couldn't restrain herself any longer, and a tirade was unleashed.

"Are you fucking kidding me?! No disrespect, but your brothers and their little band of mother-fucking merry men are the ones selling this shit. Where do you think they get all the fucking money for the jewelry, the cars, and the houses?"

Maria was eyes widened in shock. No one ever spoke outwardly about the Montenegro Doble Doble businesses. It was just understood that this topic was forbidden. She never talked about it with her brothers. She never asked Jackie what he did for them. It was a topic that was off-limits from the time she was old enough to ask questions.

"Jackie, you should know better!" Sylvia implored.

She looked at both of them, one at time, went over to the kitchen table, grabbed a pen and paper to write Father Phil's number down, and then walked out the door.

JC got the help he needed at the Montefiore program. Marking progress, he entered a halfway house where he could practice his sobriety and use his coping skills while gaining the support he needed to reenter society on his own. Everyone checked in on him from time to time, his parents, Sylvia, Jhonny, Father Phil, even Lisa Rubin.

JC AND SYLVIA, 1970

Brrring! Brrring!

The phone rang insistently in the middle of the night begging to be answered.

"Hello?" Sylvia answered, groggy from a sound sleep.

A loud curdling scream and then incessant sobbing filled the entire apartment. It startled Jamie and his siblings.

"No me digas!" (Don't tell me this!) Sylvia pleaded with the caller. She then hung up and continued her sobbing and pleading.

"Ay Dios mio! Ay Dios mio!" (Oh my God! Oh my God!) Sylvia said to no one in particular.

Not having heard the phone ring or the brief conversation, eleven-year-old Jamie had been awakened by his mother's screaming and crying and rushed to his parents' bedroom.

"Mami, what's wrong?" he asked.

"JC is dead!"

"No, no. It was just a nightmare, Mami!"

"No, mi hijo, es la verdad. JC is dead!"

Sylvia assured her son that this was the truth. JC was dead. Jamie looked at his mother in disbelief and then his father. Jhonny, still lying down in bed and rubbing Sylvia's back, nodded his head to his son, signaling that this was, in fact, true. JC is dead! His cousin, his one-time babysitter, was gone.

Jamie collapsed on the end of the bed and with tear-filled eyes asked his mother, "How? Why?"

"I don't know," she told him. "Jackie just called and said he was found by the police beneath the Unionport Bridge on Bruckner Boulevard."

"Was he mugged? Murdered?" Jamie asked, seeking an explanation.

"No, mijo. He died of an overdose," Sylvia replied plainly.

"I thought he kicked ..." Jamie's voice trailed off, his emotions tiring him out.

Sofia and Charlton piled into the room. Sylvia huddled the entire family together on the bed to tell them JC was gone. With their hearts heavy and heads bowed, the Quintana family wept together.

JC didn't die alone. Lisa Rubin, his Scarsdale girlfriend, was found next to him.

LISA RUBIN

Lisa Rubin grew up in Hartsdale, New York, a leafy suburb twenty miles north of the city. She often told people she was from Scarsdale, a neighboring town, because it was better known and carried a certain cache. A Scarsdale provenance said it all, or at least implied most of what she wanted people to know. Legend has it that in the early 1930s a Greek immigrant and ice cream salesperson named Tom Carvelas had his car break down one summer day on Central Avenue in Hartsdale. Worried that his inventory would melt, he started selling ice cream from the side of the road. It sold so well, he soon set up a roadside stand at this very site. His wares moved so fast at this site that he soon bought a plot of land nearby and opened the first Carvel Ice Cream store. Lisa realized that while fascinating, this story was less effective in conveying social status than simply stating, "I'm from Scarsdale."

Her upbringing was typical of the early fifties. Boy—her father—an intelligence officer wounded in the war, meets girl— her mother— his nurse, falls in love, marries her, and moves to the suburbs after the war. He then joined the FBI and built a good career earning a comfortable living. They had three girls, Lisa being the oldest. Her mother joined the PTA, ran the town choir, and, generally, enjoyed the fruits of the rising middle class.

Mr. Rubin, a nice Jewish boy, had married a *goy*, a Catholic. Lisa, as a dutiful daughter, attended Maria Regina High School like her mother did before her. Lisa took music lessons at the prestigious Music Conservatory of Westchester. She applied and was accepted at the New School, with a scholarship for her skills as a vocalist.

At the New School, Lisa met JC. Having not met many kids beyond her Scarsdale social circle, she assumed JC was Jewish. After all, he was tall with kinky hair. When introduced, he didn't say his last name, just gave her his nickname. She asked a friend about JC's last name.

"It's something like Cruise, I think?" the friend told her.

Lisa finally mustered the courage to ask her himself.

"JC, what's your last name?"

"Cruz," he said.

"What kind of name is that?"

"I'm Puerto Rican."

"Oh?" she said, trying to hide her surprise. "Do you speak Puerto Rican?"

JC laughed, spitting out his 7UP.

"I mean, I know that you don't speak Puerto Rican. You must speak Spanish."

JC had been passing a rehearsal hall at school when he heard a voice. The singer had turned "Summertime," an old and seductive Ella Fitzgerald tune, into a bluesy lullaby. When he looked into the room, JC couldn't believe a white girl was singing. She glanced up at him, head tilted, blue-gray eyes set close together with her light brown hair falling to one side. She was a slender girl in a white peasant shirt and bell-bottom blue jeans, and she swung slowly in bare feet as she sang. She was tan and strong looking. JC stayed until she finished her song and offered his applause. After a little conversation, they took a walk through the Village, stopping at some old record stores before JC dropped Lisa at her dorm. He left with her telephone number in his pocket. Despite the differences in upbringing, they saw a lot of themselves in each other. They both confessed to getting lost in music, reading anything they could get their hands on the subject—singers, bands, and genres—and coming to the New School with a sense of possibilities, ready to try anything.

Lisa and JC were soon taking classes, seeing avant-garde movies, and going to late-night jam sessions together in the Village and Harlem. They immersed themselves in each other and absorbed the whole counterculture in and around the Village. They had both smoked a little weed in high school and did it again the first time they made love. Soon, they experimented with other drugs together.

Lisa had a little money and access to more from her parents. It was natural that she'd score what they needed when they needed it. She always seemed to get a deal. It didn't hurt that she was an attractive young woman who could run her fingers through her hair with a come-hither smile. She and JC worked their way around a few spots in the Village, maybe a time or two in Harlem, and once or twice—just her, not him—in the Bronx. JC never wanted to go to the Bronx. He was terrified of being recognized by one of his mother's brothers or their people. He never told Lisa that his uncles moved product. But eventually, the grips of the addiction got bad enough that they would cop wherever they could.

After the rescue, Lisa parents' were in full emergency response mode. They were shocked by her appearance when they went to retrieve her from the dump in the Village. She was wraithlike, and her once mop full of hair was stringy and lifeless. They were aghast by her decline. They immediately got her to St. Vincent's Hospital in Westchester for evaluation and treatment. She gained enough strength to enter a rehab program, and she seemed to be making progress. They were relieved when she completed the program and came home.

What her parents didn't know was that she had gotten back in touch with JC as soon as she was well enough. They thought they could be stronger together and began making plans to meet each other in spots equidistant between the Bronx and Hartsdale, places like Mount Vernon, New Rochelle, and Yonkers. The slide to relapse was quick. When they met at a motel in the Bronx, near Hunts Point, she had a few bags of dope. Realizing it was not enough, they decided to cut it with whatever they could buy or steal at the local drugstore. They found themselves beneath the Unionport Bridge with their stash. The needle went in and soon the lights went out.

ORTIZ'S FUNERAL HOME

Wakes and funerals are difficult and awkward. When the services are for a twenty-one-year-old boy, the travesty is multiplied. JC's sudden death and the manner in which it happened were both tragic and deeply sorrowful. Ortiz's Funeral Home was packed each day and night for the visiting hours. Lines and lines of people—family, friends, neighbors, and classmates—came in and out of the chapel doors for hours on end. The silent shuffling and comforting hugs were occasionally punctuated with haunting outcries and wailing.

Greeting the guests in the receiving line, Jackie was stoic, while Maria was all at once deadpan and inconsolable. Sitting and praying in the chapel every day, Sylvia and her family also made time to thank those who came to pay their respects while making introductions for the mourners to the various members of the Cruz and Montenegro families. She was on and present the whole time, moving robotically from one task to the next, yet battling her rage inside, assuaging it with clenched teeth and the occasional visit to the bathroom to swallow antacids.

The Montenegro twins, both sets, came into the receiving parlor together. It was close to the end of visiting hours. They seemed to be orchestrating an entrance. Each was dressed as though he had just stepped out of a board of directors meeting trailed by a retinue of sycophants. They made their way through the crowd, respectfully kissing, hugging, and consoling aunts and cousins. They finally got in line to pay their respects to Jackie and Maria. Jackie shook their hands and accepted their hugs. The twins assumed Jackie was in shock. In fact, he was enraged—aflamed inside—but he stayed calm. He ground his teeth and clenched and unclenched his hands by his sides to siphon off the angry energy. Sylvia's warnings about the drugs and their trafficking rattled around inside his head. When he saw his mother sitting among the mourners staring empty-eyed at JC's coffin, he knew she was thinking about Ramon's end. Maria received her brothers by collapsing into their arms and beating her chest. They formed a circle around her and kept her from sinking.

Tomas, followed by Timoteo, Paolo, and Pablo, made their way over to Sylvia and Jhonny. Each bent over, kissed her cheek, shook his hand, and patted each child on the back.

"Lo siento, lo siento," they each said.

In return, Sylvia constructed the weakest fake smile she could muster, and when each was not looking, she rolled her eyes. The brothers caught her head slowly shaking from side to side. Each mistook it as Sylvia's expression of pity for the tragic loss. Their arrogance didn't allow them to see the dagger in her stare. Sylvia got up and tugged at Tomas's sleeve, pointed her chin, and gestured toward the other room. She obviously wanted a word. They left the crowded parlor of the funeral home to enter into an empty one.

"Sylvia, I'm so sorry for your loss," Tomas said yet again.

"Thank you. My brother and your sister are really hurting."

"I know. We'll take good care of them."

Sylvia nodded her head in acknowledgment of the gesture and broached the real reason for this conversation. She drew close to him in order to get his attention. Her speech was measured, clipped, quiet, but direct.

"Tomas, you and your brothers have been very good to Jackie and Maria"—she started very politely— "and I don't really give two shits about your businesses, but when one of them fucks up my family, I have a problem!"

Tomas scrunched up his face like he didn't get the reference. Sylvia continued.

"That shit you and your people sell is poison, and it kills our people—like your nephew. Of all the things you and your brothers do, and I don't know them all and don't care to know them all, but I do know this shit has to stop."

If Tomas was shocked by her affront, he didn't reveal it. He put his hands in the pockets of his neatly pressed pants. His bespoke blue jacket, held together nicely by the middle button, showed off his crisp white shirt. He rocked back and forth on the heels of his Italian loafers and thought carefully before he responded.

"Sylvia, JC was family, and whether you believe us or not, my brothers and I are truly sorry about this tragedy."

Sylvia was about to interrupt, but Tomas anticipated this and held up his immaculately manicured hand, signaling that he'd like to be heard first.

"The family is in many businesses, and the one to which you refer I can neither confirm nor deny your assertion; however, I will state that this shit, as you call it, has been around long before you and me and will remain so after we are gone. Those who supply it, do not force those who purchase it to consume it. If one enterprise exits the market, another will take its place. It is a fact of life!"

"Don't give me that crap!" Sylvia snapped back.

"Allow me to finish!" Tomas demanded.

Sylvia swept her hand in front of her as if to say, "The floor is yours."

"You and your husband smoke cigarettes, si?" Tomas did not wait for an answer as he furthered his argument.

"Smoking can kill you. In fact, I'm sure you've seen the news reports that the top doctors put out warnings of the hazards of smoking. Now, have the companies that sell these things sold any less? Did they force those who smoke to start or continue?"

Sylvia was stupefied by his logic. This man's nephew was lying in a coffin in the other room, having died of a drug overdose from drugs he probably supplied, and he was giving a lecture exonerating himself of any blame or guilt.

"Pare amigo!" Sylvia put her hand up and told Tomas to stop.

She stared straight through Tomas, wagged her finger in his face and said, "You should be ashamed of yourself! That's family lying in that coffin in the other room—your fucking nephew, your sister's oldest child! I hope JC haunts your sorry ass tonight and every night for the rest of your goddamn life!"

Sylvia then brushed by Tomas and left the room without another word.

EDWIN L. BENNETT FUNERAL HOME

A few days later, in a different funeral parlor a few miles north of the Bronx, a similar process ensued. Crowds pushed into the Edwin L. Bennett Funeral Home for hours to pay respects to the recently departed Lisa Rubin. Like Maria, Lisa's mother, Katherine, moved between periods of numbness and hysteria, all while greeting guests in the receiving line. Her father was reserved and stoic, making sure to look every mourner in the eye while shaking his or her hand. He looked very much the FBI agent in his dark suit, white shirt, and striped tie.

Sylvia had waited in line for forty-five minutes before making her way up to the Rubins, who were standing just past Lisa's closed casket. Sylvia wore a simple black dress, sensible black pumps, and a small string of pearls around her neck. She asked Jhonny to wait outside. As she approached, she saw a hint of recognition from Mel. His look suggested that he should know who she was but could not quite place her. Katherine, his wife, on the other hand, was oblivious.

"I'm so sorry for your loss. It's truly tragic," Sylvia said as she reached to clutch Katherine in a half-hug with a kiss on the cheek.

Katherine was taken aback by the familiarity, but managed a smile and nod of acknowledgement. Sylvia moved to Mel, grasped his right hand with her own, and then touched his elbow with her other hand and started to tear up.

"This is no way for a life to end," Sylvia said. "You have my sincerest sympathies."

Mel squeezed her hand in return and then in a moment of clarity took a deep breath.

"You're JC's aunt, right?"

Sylvia nodded.

"You have our sympathies as well. This is not where any of us want to be right now. It is all so senseless."

Sylvia, still holding his hand, was unable to speak at the moment, so she squeezed his hand in agreement.

"Thank you so much for coming. It means a lot to Katherine and me. I'm sorry we didn't attend JC's services. You are a better person than either of us."

"Not true. I hope you didn't mind that I came today."

"Of course not. How did you—" Mel hadn't completed his question when Sylvia answered.

"Looking through JC's things, I came across his address book and found Lisa's name and your home address listed. I wanted to pay my respects, so I called around to find where the services might be held," she explained.

"That was kind of you."

Feeling the push of the line of those wanting to pay their respects behind her, Sylvia started to leave but then turned back just slightly and said, "Special Agent Rubin, may I call your office in a week or two?"

Mel just gave her a half salute to signal his OK.

EDDY AND MEL CONTINUED

Once Mel told Eddy this new bit of information, his theory behind the motive for Sylvia's death didn't change. It just became nuanced.

"So, Sylvia pointed you in the right direction but didn't necessarily give you the map or serve as your travel guide? Help me out here," Eddy implored.

"Mrs. Q was in possession of some information but not directly. She might have been a few layers closer to the situation than we were, but her knowledge was hearsay and conjecture at best. More informed hearsay than ours but nothing that would legally help in either an investigation or a conviction. But we caught a break when another—"

"Mari Diaz?"

Mel was impressed by Eddy's investigative thoroughness.

"Yes, Mari Diaz—an assumed identity—stepped forward with more direct knowledge."

"The Mari Diaz who lived in my neighborhood?" Eddy asked.

Mel ignored Eddy's question.

"Cepeda, what I'm telling you is both off the record and not to be repeated. I will only say that you are probably correct in your assumptions around the *accident* that ended Sylvia's life. I tell you this because my visit to New York suggests that we were curious about this event as well but don't have enough to tie it together, and we don't have the resources to devote to someone's demise who was only tangential to our investigation. And, unless we had more to go on, it is also out of our jurisdiction. As much as it hurts me to say that, it is our official stance."

"Official?" Eddy asked.

"Yes. Unofficially, I'd like to nail the bastard as much as you because Sylvia meant a lot to me. She was brave and courageous, and I admired her greatly. But at this point, there is not much I can do from an investigative point of view for a lot of reasons—a big one being that I'm retired and have tried to put this painful chapter in my life behind me. My meeting with you today is to maybe ease the guilt for this official snafu and to let you know that, as best I can tell, you are getting close."

"Can I speak to this Mari Diaz?"

"In witness protection," Mel answered almost too fast.

Eddy should have seen that coming.

"I suppose this *accident* was the very reason that witness protection makes sense for our Mari Diaz?"

Mel assumed this was a rhetorical question.

"Cepeda, as a former FBI colleague, I'd tell you to leave this alone, but as a father in this drama, I hope your curiosity propels you to seek out the truth."

"Mel, I want to speak to Mari Diaz."

Mel thought about this for a second before leaning into Eddy's ear.

"Let me see if Mari is interested in talking to you."

JACKIE AND MARIA, 1971

Jackie and Maria tried to get back to their life after JC's death, but there was a veil of regret that hovered above their heads. They tended to their growing daughters as best they could, but mustering up the strength to return to the old days was sometimes too painful. It was life with doubt and second-guesses as they reran the movie of JC's upbringing. Never big drinkers, they soon started to have a cocktail each night as a way of soothing the festering wound. Each of them attended to the normal—working, making house, helping with homework, and tucking the girls into bed—but their sadness and their method of self-soothing was a weight that their daughters could hardly endure. Instinctively, the girls tried to counter the pall and add some joy in their apartment. They put on plays for their parents, built forts with the furniture cushions, and asked their parents to help slay imaginary dragons. They did all they could to coax a smile or a laugh from Maria and Jackie. When that didn't work, the girls put on a skit that imitated and parodied their parents nightly slide into an inebriated slumber. This got Jackie and Maria's attention.

Jackie knew he had to do something to change the dynamic at home. He recalled how his own mother dealt with the sudden death of her parents and how she dragged the family out to the beaches, amusement parks, and other sites around the city in an attempt to outrun the despair that had enveloped them at home. Like his mother, he wanted to help his family live out loud. Jackie took his girls to his happy place: City Island. Not only that, but he decided that life was indeed too short and uncertain, so he decided to buy a boat. Maria was shocked when he announced these plans, but Jackie said that he had set some money aside from the payments her brothers made to him for the various errands he ran for them.

It wasn't a big boat, but it wasn't small either. It was a Starcraft with an outboard motor. Comfortable for cruising and fishing, it suited Jackie's needs to get out on the water, escape the mainland, and entertain his family and friends. It was modest relative to some of the other slip owners' crafts at the boatyard, yet it still made a statement—Jackie was making a pretty good living down at Hunts Point Junk & Salvage.

Jackie liked to take his daughters and their cousins on the water. Being city kids, they were all awed by the expansiveness of the open water and the view back to the coastline. They, like him years before, all of a sudden realized how much water surrounded the Bronx and all the Boroughs. Manhattan, after all, was an island. Jackie christened his boat *Flotilla*. He remembered hearing this word during the newsreels of the war. It sounded strong. In his mind, it was a cross between *floating* and *Godzilla*, although he knew the real meaning. Sylvia and Jamie were occasional guests on the vessel. Jackie taught his nephew, along with his daughters, how to fish by tying a line, a small weight, and a hook with some bait onto the end of a beer can tab—a poor man's fishing rod. Jackie mused that these special Saturday afternoons were well worth the price of the boat. Sylvia was not so sure.

"Hermano, you enjoy this boat, si?" Sylvia asked.

"Yes, I do. Very much!"

"It doesn't bother you that this boat was paid for by the work you do for your brother-in-law?"

"Sylvia, don't ruin this. What's done is done. Let's just enjoy what we have and who we have now."

"Jackie, I don't know that I can move on like that."

"Sis, nothing and no one is ever bringing JC back," he reminded her.

"And Ramon!" Sylvia interrupted

"And Ramon, si! Living is for the living. We mourn the dead, but they're gone. Ellas se fueron!"

"Blood money, Jackie. That's what this is. They only care about you because you are married to their sister."

"Sylvia, silencio!" Jackie had enough.

He told Sylvia to be quiet and continued.

"Allow me to enjoy my family in peace. I mourn my son in silence, and I try to live my life out loud. Look at your children and mine enjoying this boat and one another. Let's leave it at that."

"Can you?"

"Sylvia, I've made my pact with these devils a long time ago when I married their sister. I'm not stupid."

"Si, hermano, si." Sylvia acquiesced.

SYLVIA AND MEL RUBIN, 1972

Sylvia took the subway uptown toward 233rd Street, near Misericordia Hospital in the Bronx. Having visited friends there before, she knew there was a drugstore down the block from the hospital that had a bank of phone booths that would offer her anonymity and privacy. In a strange way, she also thought the message to her intended would be clearer given her proximity to his home, which she knew was somewhat faulty logic in that she was actually calling his office downtown, not his home in Westchester. She wasn't thinking straight these days since she hatched the crazy idea she was about to unveil with the party she was calling. This whole plan she cooked up was wild, but she couldn't think of any other way to clean up this mess. Not for her, but for her brother and future generations. Once she opened this door, she was closing others—permanently.

Sylvia dialed the number on Mel Rubin's card. While it rang, she worried he might not remember her. After all, rather than making the call a few weeks after the services for Lisa, Sylvia had waited a few months. So unsure of what to do yet vexed by the feeling that she had to do something, Sylvia changed her mind minute to minute every day. Every day turned into months.

"Special Agent Rubin." Mel announced himself in a clipped professional voice.

"Agent Rubin, this is Sylvia Quintana, JC's aunt," she said tentatively into the phone.

"Yes, of course."

"How are you and your wife doing?"

Moving off her question, Mel responded, "How can I help you?" Special Agent Rubin was all business.

"I might have some information about the drug business that killed Lisa and JC," Sylvia explained.

After a small pause, Mel announced, "I'm listening."

"I'm sure you've heard of the Montenegro Doble Doble, correct?"

"I can't comment on that specifically, but I can say that I am aware of their existence."

"JC's father, my brother, works for them."

"Interesting."

"Jackie—that's his name—doesn't work for them directly, but he's married to a Montenegro sister and works in one of their businesses. I think he's seen some things and might be aware of others."

"Did he tell you this himself?"

"Not exactly."

"Well, not exactly is not very helpful. Does he at least know that you are making this phone call?" Mel asked.

"No, but hear me out." Sylvia continued.

"I know my brother, and he's been seething ever since JC died. He's been smart enough not to get involved in the Doble Doble, but they trust him and may have done or said things in front of him that could be useful to you all. We all know they deal in this shit, and Jackie could be helpful."

"Mrs. Quintana, your so-called knowledge around the Doble Doble's involvement in the drug trade is not enough in my business. I'm not saying it isn't directionally correct, but it's not enough."

"Special Agent Rubin, in addition to his son, Jackie and I also had a brother who died of a drug overdose, so he might be motivated to tie things together for you, directionally. I know I'm motivated."

"Mrs. Quintana, how can you be so sure of both your brother's knowledge and his motivation?"

"Tomas, the real leader of the Doble Doble, has always taken to Jackie. He's always down at the shop talking with Jackie and with others in Jackie's company. I know Tomas, and he's arrogant enough to believe that Jackie doesn't pay attention. And his trust is misplaced in Jackie's loyalty, especially after JC's death."

"Assuming all that you've said is true, how would you suggest setting up a meet with Jackie?" Mel questioned.

"I have an idea of how to get my brother to the table," Sylvia responded. "But you have to leave me out of it."

"Why?"

"Jackie has always been on his own. Being my older brother, he may hear me, but he sometimes has a hard time listening to me. What do they call it in the political process? I can provide the propaganda to help influence his thinking, but you have to get him to vote your way with a little influence of your own."

"How so?"

"With leverage." Sylvia said Judas-like.

JACKIE AND THE FBI, 1972

Jackie was walking down Randall Avenue toward his shop. He had just returned from retrieving his lunch and making a deposit at the bank when a shiny black sedan stopped right next to him. The driver, tall, clean-cut, and wearing dark sunglasses and a dark suit got out and flashed a badge. He asked Jackie to get in the back seat next to another clean-cut gentleman. Jackie looked around and hesitated, almost expecting the *Candid Camera* crew to pop out somewhere.

"Mr. Cruz, we are with the FBI. I've asked you politely and discreetly to get into the car."

Jackie looked back at the driver and ducked into the car. The car took off from the curb and drove deliberately toward the Bronx River and an out-of-the-way vacant parking lot. During the ride, not a word was spoken. Jackie was too frightened to say or ask anything. Each of the agents—there were three, two up front one in the back—sat stoned-faced behind their dark shades and stared straight ahead. When the car finally stopped, the passenger in the back next to Jackie turned to face him.

"Joaquin Cruz, we are special agents with the local FBI. You are not under arrest; however, we'd like to have a conversation with you about your business and your business associates."

Jackie was careful to remain calm and unaltered so as not to have his facial expression or body language betray any of the trepidation he felt. He did not say anything. Jackie just sat there.

"OK, so you're not one for talking right now. So, why don't you just listen."

"If I'm not under arrest, why don't I get out right here," Jackie responded. "I don't have to listen…"

"No you don't, but I'd suggest you hear what I have to say about you and your wife, Maria."

Jackie sat more upright.

"Mr. Cruz, we know that you have worked at the Hunts Point Junk & Salvage for many years. We know that you have a modest apartment with your wife, Maria—who doesn't work—and your three daughters. You had an older son, now deceased."

"All correct. What's your point?" Jackie stated somewhat impatiently.

"Oh, I'm getting to the point, Mr. Cruz. You and your wife, Maria, don't own a car but you do own a boat that you keep in City Island. This boat, at retail, is a rather large purchase given your reported earnings, is it not?"

"I—" Jackie started.

"Mr. Cruz, it was a rhetorical question. We already know the answer to that. Given what we know about you and the job at your shop, there is no way you could afford that boat. Records indicate that you did not receive any inheritance or any insurance proceeds from any relative who may have passed. Furthermore, you have not been the lucky winner of any lotteries. However, records do indicate that your wife is a Montenegro."

"So?"

"So, her brothers are the leaders of a reputed syndicate called the Montenegro Doble Doble. They are allegedly involved in many illegal activities—some of which we believe occur at your shop. All such activities generate a lot of cash. Does my logic compute so far?"

"I don't know what you are talking about. I've saved for many years to buy that boat. And if any of this were true, you would have busted the Montenegro brothers already."

"Well, let me respond to your statements one at a time." The agent continued.

"You bought that boat with cash—not with a check, not with a credit card, but with green dollars. These dollars were not withdrawn from a bank of any kind. Perhaps your brothers-in-law have been generous to you for reasons other than just running their little junk shop. How am I doing so far? Again, rhetorical. No need to answer. Allow me to continue. The fact is that your sister's brothers are *definitely* engaged in these activities. That much is true. You are correct in that we haven't been able to bust them because they are careful and haven't left us any hard evidence to tie them to their crimes. So, let's agree that the crimes have occurred but the busts have not. At least, not yet."

"I'm not saying anything about my brothers-in-law because I don't know anything. I do know that I have not committed any crimes."

"True. You have not directly been involved in any criminal activities, but the boat and the cash would suggest that you and Maria are the beneficiaries of the fruits of such activities. And perhaps the fact that when your shop closes at night, the lights remain on while a parade of cars go in and out all night suggests that your facility is being used by your brothers-in-law. And they provide a certain—how do you say— *propina*, or tip for your cooperation."

Jackie didn't know if he should admit that the brothers owned the shop through one of their corporations. Wouldn't that make it their right to do with it what they please? Or was this beside the point? The agent's use of Maria's name rattled Jackie. While he might be able to take the heat, he wasn't so sure she was equipped to do the same.

"Mr. Cruz, I can tell by your silence you are deliberating on your options here, so let me be clear. If you choose not to assist us, which is your right, we plan on bringing charges against you and Maria for failure to report all sources of income, falsifying your tax returns, and general tax evasion. This could result in forfeiture of any of your possessions or jail time or both. It will certainly ruin any reputation you have, it will most certainly make your daughters' lives a bit more difficult, and it will make it difficult to gain employment later on, unless you work for your brothers-in-law, who don't seem to care about such matters."

"What do my taxes have to do with any of this?"

"Not much really, but it is what we have right now. Oh, by the way, you may think your brothers-in-law are running a little chop shop out of your place because of the vehicle traffic at night, but we have reason to believe that these vehicles have traveled across state lines with drugs stuffed into the paneling, which makes it Federal. And, for the record, taxes brought down Al Capone."

Jackie tried to think of a quick retort.

"Well, if you're so smart, why don't you charge my brothers-in-law with all the same things and make the same threats to them?"

"Because they have better accountants and lawyers than you do!"

Jackie just grunted.

"Mr. Cruz, for your own safety, we are going to ask you to get out here and find your way back to your shop. You can blame your tardiness on a bank error or delay in your deposits today.

Yes, we've been watching you. And we'd like you to think about your cooperation with us as a get-out-of-jail-free card for you and Maria. We just need some information, and we'd shield you so it would never come back to you. Make sense?"

Jackie mouthed the word *si* without expending any breath.

"One last thing. I'd keep this conversation to yourself for a multitude of reasons. Not even a word of it to Maria. Again, for your safety, don't reach out to us. We'll be in touch with you shortly."

It irritated Jackie that the agent kept on using his wife's name, but he figured that was exactly the point—to intentionally get under his skin. He got out of the car. The driver closed the door, rolled up the windows, locked all the doors, and departed the parking lot as though he had just dropped off a friend after work.

Jackie couldn't sleep that night. His mind was racing, and he had the cold sweats. Maria asked him what was wrong. Jackie blamed his restlessness and his profuse sweating on a bad meal at lunch. Every lie had some semblance of truth attached. He got up and went into his living room. Jackie poured himself a tumbler of scotch. He sat in his easy chair and wondered what he should do next. Aside from rustling his family in the middle of the night, asking them to gather their belongings, and running away—which wasn't very practical—Jackie boiled his options down to three things. Go to his brothers-in-law and tell them what happened. With their lawyers and accountants, maybe they could get him out of this mess or help them run away. He could go talk to Sylvia. She had always been a survivor with good instincts. She might offer a way out or a least a way to think of a way out. Lastly, he could just cooperate and let the chips fall where they may. The FBI said they could ... What was the phrase? Shield them from it coming back to him. Jackie took a sip of scotch and felt its smooth burn from inside his mouth. He closed his eyes and tried to think. His brothers-in-law, his sister, or the FBI?

The sun slipping in from the windows of his living room woke Jackie in his easy chair. The now nearly empty bottle on the table and the broken glass on the floor told him that he had finally passed out from the combination of the alcohol and the mental exhaustion. He awakened with some clarity, as though his subconscious had wrestled with the choices and narrowed it down for him. Sylvia was levelheaded but had an axe to grind against his wife's family because of the deaths of both JC and Ramon. She couldn't be counted on to be objective in this decision. The FBI had a hammer, and he was the nail. They were going to pound on its head until they drove it into place. His brothers-in-law had always been good to him and kept him away from the specifics of their business, but Jackie couldn't pretend not to imagine the extent of their various dealings. In the abstract, he could claim ignorance, but deep down, he knew who they were and what they did.

He had known the brothers all his life. From an early age, Jackie had witnessed their relentlessness in either persuading or pushing others to see things their way. They were brutal, they were greedy, and they sought dominance no matter who was in the way. The Doble Doble always strove for more business and more profitable enterprises. There was always collateral damage, but Tomas believed in the concept of acceptable casualties—something he had picked up from watching the war documentaries. The bigger the battles and the prizes to be won, the bigger the tally of MIAs and KIAs. While he never said it aloud, Jackie believed that Tomas viewed JC as an acceptable casualty. He remembered Tomas at the wake and the funeral. He mourned sufficiently, he had the right measure of empathy, but he never took any responsibility, not even coincidentally. Tomas mourned not for JC, not for Jackie. He was there because of his sister, Maria. Everyone else was incidental. Again, Jackie imagined how Tomas distanced himself and his drug dealing from these events. The drug trade was their biggest and most profitable business. While he didn't push the needle, his people and his network pushed the poison. Still, Jackie knew his newfound courage was the aftermath of the alcohol and the bright sunshine that filled the room. The reality was that the Doble Doble were a fucking scary bunch. What was the saying? You can pick your friends, but you can't pick your relatives. Like it or not, the DDs were Maria's family. Jackie wasn't looking forward to the next visit with the FBI.

That visit never happened. Jackie died in an accident at Hunts Point Junk & Salvage about a week later. Interestingly, he was said to have had a little too much to drink and slipped into a piece of very dangerous machinery that was used to demolish automobiles. It crushed Jackie to death. No one was around to either witness the event or save him. His body was discovered a few hours later by one of the yard's employees who was coming in for the night shift. The authorities, after a brief investigation, confirmed it as a tragic accident.

ORTIZ'S FUNERAL HOME—JACKIE

Maria seemed to be catatonic. Her face was expressionless, and her eyes were bloodshot. She appeared lost and confused, and her movements were all in slow motion. Sylvia had to hold Maria's hand and guide her movements as mourners approached to offer their condolences. Her mind had obviously abandoned her, while her body carried on firmly planted in the reception line at Ortiz's Funeral Home beside Jackie's closed casket. Sylvia was directing traffic for those who stood in line for hours. She asked her eldest son, Jamie—all of twelve years old—to act as a sheepdog, keeping the crowds moving uniformly toward the widow. Stolid in his responsibility, he pointed to where each should stand, kneel, and wait their turn. The mourners all approached the family—Maria and her daughters—with dread and an awful feeling of déjà vu, having run this same gauntlet for JC's services.

"Ay que lastima!"

Friends and relatives recounted one way or another that it was such a pity for tragedy to revisit this family. They held Maria close, they hugged the girls tightly, and they whispered prayers to God.

"Ay Dios mio!"

Sylvia heard Maria murmur, "Why me? Why us? I can't do this again. No! No!"

"Maria, you need to be strong for your girls," Sylvia whispered to her sister-in-law.

Orchestrating the masses from across the room, Sylvia moved Jamie with her eyes toward stragglers and the others who were stepping out of line to greet long-forgotten friends in the chapel. Sylvia needed to maintain some semblance of order in this crowd in order to keep Maria relatively calm. She knew her sister-in-law's emotions were raw and her nerves on the verge of exploding. Jamie was being strong for his mother and executing his duties as she commanded, but he too was filled with emotion and confusion. His mother was being dutiful, but her pain and anger were palpable in the deepened lines on her forehead.

Sylvia was deeply saddened, but her furor took precedence in her mood. Sharing in the loss of her nephew JC and now her brother Jackie, Sylvia too had reason to climb into that dark place of misery and allow it to swallow her whole; however, she learned over the years to gather herself and put that negative energy toward survival. Her survival instincts mixed with her feelings of guilt for having put Jackie in harm's way were brewing within. For some odd reason, as she digested this noxious cocktail of anger, survival, and guilt, Sylvia seemed to recall the first law of physics that stated: An object at rest stays at rest, and an object in motion stays in motion with the same speed and in the same direction unless acted upon by an unbalanced force. In this unlikely contemplation, Sylvia realized that Jackie was the object and her efforts created the unbalanced force that cost him his life.

Just then, the Montenegro brothers made their entrance. Jamie always felt a shiver run up his spine when they appeared at functions. He couldn't quite understand why they had this effect on him, especially Tomas. He was always perfectly quaffed and pedicured, the picture of calm, cool, and control. Yet, Jamie swore that he saw a tempest swelling in Tomas's eyes. To Jamie, Tomas's dark eyes simultaneously told stories and held secrets. They had their own unique language, intricate, seductive, and destructive all at once. As a twelve-year-old, Jamie didn't know how to process these feelings of repulsion and intrigue all at once. He was frightened and dared not lock eyes with Tomas.

The Montenegro brothers moved around the room greeting relatives and soothing the grief-stricken. They approached Maria and her girls and enveloped them all in a group hug of condolence.

Maria shrieked, cried and stomped her feet, "No! No! No! My Jackie. My Jackie. No! No! No!"

The boys tried to console her in a chorus of "Sh! Sh!"

Sylvia simmered as she witnessed this charade. Tomas glanced Sylvia's way as though he wanted to make sure that she knew he was there or to measure her reaction to this show of support. He broke free while still looking at Sylvia. He reached inside his pristine midnight-blue jacket and pulled out a small bottle from the inside pocket. Tomas approached Jackie's casket, stopped for effect, and looked around before lifting the lid ever so slightly. He gave a long glance at the bottle—which appeared to be the hot sauce that Jackie always seemed to slather on his meal—and then slowly placed it inside near the lifeless body before bringing the lid down.

Tomas walked over to Sylvia and bent in to kiss her cheek, but she recoiled. This caught Tomas off guard, but then he smiled, nodded his head, and began to speak.

"Sylvia, it is truly awful that such a tragedy visits Maria once again. And because he's your brother, you too share in this pain. Lo siento!"

Sylvia stood there motionless, blinking back her fury. She was just amazed at the fucking balls on this guy. Unable to stay in character as a respectful relative, Sylvia remained mute.

Tomas felt the need to fill in the void.

"I've known Jackie a long time—a good, long time. Coming up together and having him work the shop. It pains me that he's gone, especially because it happened at the shop."

"Bullshit!" Sylvia couldn't contain herself any longer.

"Perdona me?" Tomas feigned confusion.

"While Jackie ran the shop all these many years, there were never any accidents or tragedies. Now he slips and falls into that machine and dies? And while he's alone? *Please!* Spare me!"

Tomas, ready to spar, responded.

"Sylvia, it grieves me to no end that this should happen at our place together. If that machine were a dog that had mauled him, I would put it down immediately! It's all our pain but still a tragic set of circumstances."

Sylvia, mindful of her environment, closed in on Tomas and pointed her finger in the middle of his chest.

"Tomas, we've been here before. Your act of contrition and support are all forgotten after you leave here and wipe your sister's tears off your lapels."

Tomas's face finally betrayed his own anger. He stepped closer and stared down at Sylvia, his lips curling tightly around his teeth.

Just then, Jamie stepped between them, facing his mother.

"Mom, Titi Maria needs you!"

Sylvia moved her eyes from her son up to Tomas. She turned and exited from the confrontation. But then stopped suddenly and turned back to Tomas.

"You'll get yours," she said.

Jamie, keeping his back to Tomas, looked over his left shoulder at Tomas and then quickly walked away.

"Mom, what were you saying to Uncle Tomas?" Jamie inquired

"Oh, it was nothing. He did something that upset me. And you know me and my big mouth. I had to say something to him. Not to worry, mijo," Sylvia responded, pulling her son in for a hug.

"And he's really not your uncle," She added with pleasure.

"He's kind of scary."

"Yes, he is mi hijo. Yes, he is."

EDDY AND THE DEVIL

Eddy was zipping up the FDR Drive heading toward the Willis Avenue Bridge in his rental car when his phone buzzed. The caller ID said the number was private, which led him to debate whether he should answer or let it go to voicemail. If it went to voicemail, he reasoned quickly, the caller may not leave a message. In addition, because he was cautious about giving his number out, one could assume it was someone he knew or someone one of his contacts thought he should know. He gave into the impulse to answer the phone.

"Cepeda," Eddy barked into the phone.

"Hermano, I'm hurt. You come into town from PR, and you don't call, you don't write, you don't visit. What am I to think?"

Eddy knew the voice, but he couldn't quite place it. The accent and the inflection were familiar to him, but he couldn't quite land a name. Rather than betray his ignorance, he played along.

"Had I known you were around, I would have baked a cake and brought it to you or at least made some flan."

"Well, I will give you a chance to make up since you've seemed to have checked in with others from the hood."

Eddy took the hint. Whoever this was, knew he was in town, knew he had talked to some people, and got his telephone number.

"How do I get my chance?" Eddy asked.

"Why don't you meet me for una cafe, Special Agent Cepeda?" The caller teased out the salutation.

Eddy now had an idea who it was that was baiting him. There weren't many people from his circle who cared that he was FBI, and there weren't many people who would have the power or resources to know his whereabouts and find his mobile number. Eddy was now speaking to Tomas Montenegro, the devil himself.

"*Retired* Special Agent, Tomas. You should know that."

"Perdona me. I do know that you have since hung up your shield, but maybe not your instincts."

Eddy let that comment pass without a response.

Tomas continued.

"Since you are very well acquainted with the life of a Boricue, living on Isla Verde and all, let's see how the others live, shall we? Meet me at Prince Coffee House on Arthur Avenue con los Italianos." Tomas broke out in Spanglish. "It's near Fordham University. We can have espresso and cannoli. Let's say in an hour."

"Si ... y gracias" Eddy responded.

"Prego!" Tomas answered in Italian.

The call was terminated. Tomas had reached out, delivered his message, and asked for a meet. Eddy knew what this cat-and-mouse charade was all about. Tomas wanted to know what Eddy knew. Eddy wanted to see why Tomas was so interested in a retired special agent's movements.

Eddy stepped into the very hip Prince Coffee House on Arthur Avenue in the Bronx's Little Italy. It had a multitude of windows on a large garage door displayed on each side. Small round tables and teak chairs were laid out beneath a very large, chic chandelier. It was a very public place, not at all where he expected Tomas to set up a meeting. Perhaps, the setting was a message that he had nothing to hide.

Tomas was already seated at one of the round tables. Eddy had not laid eyes on him in years. The grainy photos of Tomas from the FBI files were many years old. Tomas's frame was prison-hard, and the clean-shaven head and goatee look with the aviator sunglasses came right out of central casting. The leather jacket, white T-shirt, blue jeans, and leather loafers without socks completed the look. He looked relaxed and anything but his age, which was several decades beyond the half-century mark. True to his word, an espresso and a cannoli were set on the table before him.

"Eddy, please come join me."

He extended his hand, which Eddy reluctantly shook and immediately flashed to the scene in *It's a Wonderful Life* when Jimmy Stewart, playing George Bailey, realizes he's shaking the detestable Mr. Potter's hand and slowly withdraws it in disgust. He resisted the temptation to do the same here, not wanting to provoke Lucifer incarnate.

"Would you like anything? Una cafe?" Tomas asked.

"No, thank you. I'm fully caffeinated"

Eddy scanned the room quickly and noticed that Tomas had brought reinforcements. There were two guys sitting just behind and to the right of Tomas. Their sheer girth and ugliness suggested more brawn than brains. One held a frozen scowl. The other looked like all his teeth had been pulled out and then put back out of order. The bulges that upset the lines of their not-so-pressed jackets also hinted at their job descriptions: personal protection—bodyguards.

"Eddy, Eddy, Eddy. What brings you back to New York? I understand you have a fairly nice life in Isla Verde."

"Can't a brother come back home every once in a while?"

"Of course! But weren't you back recently for Sylvia Quintana's services?"

"You keeping tabs?" Eddy questioned.

"No, just observant," Tomas said. "How is Jamie or Gordo as you call him?"

"He's fine. Still grieving the loss of his moms and taking care of his extended family. Your nieces, no?"

"Si. Although I haven't seen them in years, being away and all. While I was away, they didn't even call or write. Can you believe that?"

"Kids lead busy lives these days."

Such were the opening salvos of this conversation, which, in reality, was a mutual interrogation. Tomas and Eddy were trading light blows, seeking an opening to exploit.

"Eddy, when are you heading back to the island?"

"You trying to get rid of me? I just got here for our little meet. Here's your hat. What's your hurry?"

"Amigo, I am in town only a short time, just attending to details of my many business interests. You know, tying up all the loose ends."

Eddy didn't know if should admire Tomas's hutzpah or punch the fucking guy in the mouth. The big uglies over Tomas's shoulder tempered Eddy's reaction.

"Must be a lot of loose ends, given your absence from the day-to-day management of the business."

Tomas smiled at Eddy's verbal repartee.

"Si. Eddy, New York is no longer my home—too fast for me. I'm not a puppy anymore. So, I'm off to my little hacienda in Costa Rica. Warmer climate and less prying eyes, but I wanted to see you before I left and impart some of the wisdom I've accumulated over the years."

"Por que? Am I a loose end that needs tending?"

"Eddy, as a former special agent, you should know that among the alleged talents I have is the ability to make people disappear, or so the authorities believe. If you were an inconvenience, some believe I could simply snap my fingers"—Tomas snapped his fingers for effect—"and make you disappear. No, I've asked you here to share some of my hard-earned wisdom, claro?"

Eddy gave Tomas a 'why not' shrug of his shoulders granting his permission for the old man to proceed with his so-called lesson.

"Señor FBI, I think that you are chasing ghosts that were never alive to begin with. There are conspiracy theories spun like *narcocorridos*, those little drug ballads, intended to entertain and pump up someone's reputation, which are far from the truth. Whatever it is you're doing back in New York, I hope it doesn't involve me. Because I will tell you, it is a waste of your time."

Eddy was amazed at how much bullshit Tomas could spew, as though he were an attorney hired to obscure and gloss over the facts in order to confuse the jury. And Eddy wasn't sure if the *disappear* comment was a veiled threat to him or to Gordo or to them both.

"Are you threatening me?" Eddy asked.

Tomas threw up his hands as he rocked back in his chair and said with a laugh, "Eddy, you misunderstand my words. Point being is that between law enforcement and what you hear on the streets, one would think that I have been involved in everything from Kennedy's assassination to the Lindbergh kid's kidnapping to the untimely deaths of my brother-in-law way back when and his sister's recently. All these insinuations are unfounded and simply not true—not to mention, hurtful to me."

"Uh-huh."

"I just don't want you spending your time looking into things that have no basis in reality."

"How do you know I'm looking into anything at all?" Eddy asked.

"Well, the one talent my brothers and I do possess and will admit to is that we do have a lot of eyes and ears in and around these parts—old friends, people who feel tight with us. And for whatever reason, since we got out, people like to tell us if they see or hear anything unusual. You coming to New York and asking a lot of questions is unusual. Just saying."

"Tomas, don't flatter yourself. If I am asking questions, and I'm not suggesting that I am, they may not concern you at all. After all, you were the one who sought me out. In my former line of work, if I wanted to know something about you, I would have approached you to see how you'd react and how you'd either answer or evade my questions. As you know, I've not sought an audience with you, but you have with me."

"Cute. Very cute, Retired Special Agent Cepeda. Well, then I guess we have nothing to discuss since you don't have questions for me, and I, misunderstanding your movements, thought I could save you some time."

Tomas's ability to separate business from family was truly remarkable. In his dark mind, they occupied two different worlds, one walled off from the other. His ability to speak without emotion about Jackie's death—and, by association, the death of his sister Maria and the scattering of her children—and Sylvia's death spoke to his black heart.

"Tomas, since you asked me here, I do have a question for you, if I may?"

With a turned-down smirk on his face and a shrug of his shoulders while holding his arms out with his hands turned up, Tomas seemed to say, "Why not?"

"Why did you deposit a particular bottle of picante hot sauce into Jackie's coffin during his viewing at Ortiz's?"

"Amigo, you should know better. This is one of the traditions of our people," Tomas proceeded to preach. "When you die, those who are close to you and remember you bring you a gift to take with you to the other side. It is typically something that is small but something that brought the deceased great pleasure in this life. Ever since I've known Jackie—and that's a long time—he loved that hot sauce. He always had a bottle down at the yard and put it on everything he ate—eggs in the morning, hot dogs, hamburgers, and especially on rice and beans."

"From what I heard, it was a special brand, si?"

"Yes! Jackie got it special. I think from our old neighborhood in Spanish Harlem."

"Where did *you* get the bottle you placed inside Jackie's coffin?"

"Retired Special Agent Cepeda ..." Tomas drew out the appellation slowly and syllabically either for emphasis or irritation.

"I thought you said you had a question, not a series of questions. And before I answer any more, which is not to say that I will, what exactly are you going to do with the information if I provide it to you?"

"Tomas, I thought we were having a friendly catchup. Strike my last question and let me make a statement. A bottle of this exact same hot sauce was mailed to Jamie before Sylvia's *accident*."

Now it was Eddy who was drawing out this last word slowly and syllabically.

"It appeared to have been sent from Sylvia herself with a mysterious note saying: 'like brother, like son.' In my former line of work, we call that a clue and a threat."

Tomas, again, shrugged his shoulders, extended his arms with his palms facing up, and shook his head in an attempt at tacit denial. He leaned in toward Eddy and asked a question in a professorial manner.

"Retired Special Agent Cepeda, have you ever heard the expression Sangre por Sangre?" Tomas queried Eddy on the "blood for blood" oath.

"Si. Why do you ask?"

"No reason. It's just something that came to my mind."

"Tomas, if we're keeping score at home, you are way ahead in the body count. Muy sangre aqui, no?"

Tomas did not respond to Eddy's inquiry about bodies and blood.

Eddy got up from the table, excused himself without shaking hands, and left Tomas with his espresso and half-eaten cannoli. He thought he should change rental cars immediately in case Tomas's crew might have secured trackers to the undercarriage of his car.

EDDY AND MARI

Eddy checked the address he was texted against the number he stared at on the building before him and the street sign that hung off the pole. This looked like the place. He read the text again. It said that the building was on Jane Street in the West Village right near West Street. With one last 360-degree sweep around, Eddy determined he was in the right place. In addition, he had taken mental notes of people or vehicles taking a particular interest in his coming to this address. His knew he had not been followed. He was having difficulty reconciling the person he was looking for with this bohemian neighborhood. Perhaps she had been here forever while the world around got younger, hipper, and more expensive. He scanned the names on the labels next to the apartment buzzers. Eddy found the name he was looking for and pressed the buzzer: Rubin.

The voice of an older woman answered and asked who was calling in her native tongue.

"Quien eres?"

"Senorita, yo soy Eddy Cepeda from the old neighborhood" Eddy replied in his best Spanglish.

"Mr. All-American FBI?" the woman asked.

Her quick categorization of his life caught Eddy off guard.

"Si," he replied.

"What do you want?"

"Special Agent Mel Rubin told me where I could find you. May I come up?"

Eddy's reply was met with a long silence. She asked him to look up at the camera in the lobby and hold up some ID as well. He was about to repeat his request to come up when the door buzzed open. He glanced at the label for the apartment number—11F—headed to the elevator, and pressed the button for the eleventh floor. He got off and headed toward 11F. The door was slightly ajar. When he appeared in full in front of the door, what he saw—no, who he saw—took his breath away. Eddy grabbed at his chest with his right hand and steadied himself by placing his left hand on the doorframe as he bent over in disbelief.

He was physically rocked by who stood across from him inside of the doorway. He was staring at a ghost. Mari Diaz was the former Maria Cruz, born Maria Montenegro.

Maria was dead—or so everyone believed. Looking at her closely, Eddy realized that time had treated her kindly. Her hair was still as dark as ink, though with slight silver streaks here and there. The brown eyes were still soft. She was smaller than Eddy remembered, perhaps shrunken by age or sorrow. Eddy could tell she was sizing him up, trying to reconcile the full-grown man before her with the memory of the college boy she probably remembered.

"Mrs. Cruz—may I call you that?"

She nodded, and he continued.

"I hate to bother you, but Special Agent Rubin ... Wow. Oh my God." Eddy, still unsteady, asked if they could sit down.

Once seated with a glass of water in his hands, Eddy began again to tell her why he was there. But before he could continue, Maria spoke.

"Mel told me you have been persistent in your inquiries. Before he gave you the name of Mari Diaz, he had suggested that I decline. I told Mel that I'm too old to run again. And whatever has passed, has passed. Time to come out of the shadows. Mel has been so good to me. He knows that if the story is to be told, it is mine to tell, and I want to tell it. I need to unburden my soul to someone other than the authorities, and Mel trusts you. That's why he gave you Mari."

"Special Agent Rubin mentioned that there was an informant from the old neighborhood who was familiar with Montenegro Doble Doble and became instrumental in the investigation to put them away. But I was not expecting *you*. *You* ... died!"

Maria got a chuckle from that last bit.

"Was that funny? It wasn't intended to be," said Eddy.

"Well, the *familiar* part of Agent Rubin's description was a little play on words. Because the informant was indeed *familia* to the Doble Doble. And yes, Maria Montenegro Cruz died back then."

"Indeed."

"Eddy, I grew up the oldest in that Montenegro family. I watched as my brothers created and grew their little gang from local street hustlers to what I came to acknowledge way too late was a large criminal enterprise. My husband, Jackie, and I were childhood sweethearts. We both just got along to get along with the whole thing. Somehow we kidded ourselves that they were still just some street ruffians."

"But they were your family."

"Precisely. And I blindly believed in their goodness because they were always good to me and Jackie. I didn't see or didn't

167

care to see if there were any consequences to what they were involved in because it didn't involve me or Jackie, really. Then all of a sudden, it did. When JC died."

"Lo siento! That must have been hard."

"The worst. I was ... We were devastated! JC was such a good kid, loved his music, off to college in the Village, and the whole thing. When he first collapsed and called for help, we were shocked and caught off guard. I guess we were in a little denial too. But the rehab worked—or so we thought. And then he overdosed."

Maria suddenly got quiet. Eddy could tell that she was replaying that tragedy in her mind. She started to tear up, and her voice shook as she picked up the narrative.

"I was numb the whole time during his wake, at his funeral, and for months afterward. Jackie and I were walking zombies. My poor girls, JC's sisters, didn't know how to act. I could tell they were cautious around us, and then they decided it was their job to try to cheer us up. By then, Jackie and I were drowning our sorrows a little too much. We weren't drunks, but we definitely were trying not to feel. It was too hard, too painful!"

"Then Jackie died too," Eddy interjected.

"Yes, but there was so much more leading up to that time. We finally got our footing back after the girls gently let us know that maybe we were not being ideal parents. It was not finger-pointing but some make believe that they shared with us that hit too close to home. So Jackie and I started taking the girls out. Jackie loved City Island and on a whim bought a boat. He loved that boat, and it brought him and the girls so much joy to share it with our family and friends. And the boat ultimately brought you here today."

At that last statement, Eddy turned his head sideways like he was straining to hear.

Maria smiled and patted his hand.

"Jackie was always careful not to get involved in my brother's business. They asked him to do small, what appeared to be harmless, favors. Nothing that smelled bad to us. And they always took care of us financially. Aside from Jackie's salary at the yard, they gave him a little cash here and there for the errands he ran for them. Jackie never spent any of that cash. He kept saying he'd save if for a rainy day. And then he bought the boat with some of that cash. The FBI showed up shortly thereafter and threatened him with tax evasion unless he snitched."

"Did he?"

"No."

"Then how and why are you here?"

"Jackie was so rattled by the visit from the FBI that he was restless and couldn't sleep for days. They swore him to secrecy, but Jackie was always a gentle and sincere soul. He couldn't wrestle this thing himself."

"So he told his sister Sylvia!" Eddy blurted out, wanting to finish her thought and complete the circle.

"No, he told me."

"I don't understand."

"Jackie came to me one night, visibly shaken. He was crying like an inconsolable baby. I was in bed. I thought he was working late, but he told me that he had been walking around the Bronx most of the night, heavy with this thing. 'What thing?' I asked him. He told me about the visit from the FBI and their ultimatum. He didn't know what to do. He wanted my opinion. After all, they were my brothers."

"What did you tell him?"

"Well, we first talked about what we could do. Talk to Sylvia and get her take. I didn't think that made sense because Jackie and I both knew what she'd suggest. And as much as we both loved and respected her, that wouldn't work because she was hell-bent on the drug thing. Tell my brothers and allow them to help us in some way maybe, but I was afraid of my brothers and wasn't sure they'd put us first. Jackie had seen what they did to their people who screwed up. And it was Jackie's buying the boat that brought Fed attention. They would view that as a screw up. So we passed there as well."

"So Jackie went to the Feds?"

"No. We decided to think on it and maybe pray on it, although neither of us were particularly religious, but it seemed like the appropriate time to invoke some religion. Jackie said we needed a Hail Mary, whatever that meant, so we did nothing for the moment."

"OK."

Maria took her time to unwind this tale slowly. It seemed a cathartic exercise for her, as though she were exorcising the demons that had accumulated over the years.

"Then Jackie died in that accident at the yard." She continued. "Supposedly, he had a little too much to drink and wandered out by the car compactor. It was activated, and he fell in and died. It was strange that no one was around in the yard at the time. So he never did snitch for the Feds."

"So you didn't think it was an accident?"

"It was an execution!"

"But why?"

Maria looked away.

"From what I have come to know, Jackie was spotted getting out of that FBI sedan down by the Bronx River by one of the Doble Doble street slingers. This piece-of-shit, lowlife dealer was working the corner when he thought he saw Jackie get out of this black car. He saw the three guys in suits in the car and put it all together. Looking to score some points, he told his boss, and eventually, it got back to my brothers."

She paused again, looking down at her hands in her lap as she summoned the will to continue to unpack this history.

"So again, the story goes that the Doble Doble was on high alert and started working their snitches and their people on the inside of law enforcement and came away with enough to believe that Jackie was compromised."

"Did they ever bring it up to you or Jackie?"

Eddy saw a tear or two slowly slide down from Maria's eye and streak her face. Eddy offered her a handkerchief, which she waved off.

"Judge and jury, they decided. And I believe it was Tomas who said that he was a liability, and they killed him, making it look like an accident."

"Did you confront Tomas or any of your brothers?" Eddy asked.

"How could I? At the time, remember, while I knew about the FBI, I could never conceive that my brothers would kill my husband. Never. I just thought our family was snakebitten. Another tragic accident to endure."

"When did your mind change?"

"When Sylvia came to apologize to me after Jackie's funeral."

"Why apologize?"

"She said she brought this on us. You see, she was the first one to approach the FBI. As you know, Special Agent Rubin was Lisa Rubin's father, JC's girlfriend at school. Sylvia met Rubin when she rescued JC and Lisa from their first overdose. He gave her his card at that time. Months later, when JC and Lisa overdosed and died together, Sylvia was so angry. Drugs had taken her brother Ramon and now her nephew. She blamed my family and the Doble Doble, so she reached out to Agent Rubin."

Eddy didn't move as Maria continued.

"She told Mel what she thought she knew about my brothers' operation and their part in the drug trade. Her knowledge was all secondhand, but she offered up her brother Jackie's cooperation because he was on the inside."

"I don't get it."

"Sylvia told Mel that she couldn't ask Jackie directly for his cooperation because she knew that he wouldn't want to get involved, but if the FBI had leverage on him, he'd do the right thing. The cash for the boat was the leverage."

"Is that how it went down?"

"Sort of. Sylvia negotiated Jackie's deal without his knowledge. She told them that she would give the FBI the leverage to apply to Jackie only if he got immunity and only if he was offered a way to give the goods without having to testify. She also told them in no uncertain terms that Jackie could never know that she was providing the tips."

"Did they go for it?"

"They had been tracking my brothers for years and didn't have anything concrete on them. Mel Rubin became a hero when he came in with a potential CI. You see, Jackie and I were part owners of Hunts Point Junk & Salvage. The FBI could use this to witness the after-hours activities at the yard. It was a big break in their investigation. They accepted Sylvia's terms and approached Jackie."

"But he died before he could cooperate." Eddy jumped in.

"Yes, but I took the deal instead."

"What?"

"I was angry! I knew in my heart that Jackie didn't die in an accident. When Sylvia came to me shortly after the funeral and sat me down in confidence and told me everything about how she approached the FBI, I was even angrier. As I said, she was so sorry, so apologetic, and felt so guilty. At first, I was really pissed, but I realized that she didn't kill Jackie. She didn't kill JC. My brothers had a hand in both of their deaths. I eventually told Sylvia that I forgave her and wanted to know how I could get in touch with the FBI. Under the ruse of going for a drive in the country, we both drove to Special Agent Rubin's house where I told him that I would be their CI."

"What happened then?"

"Sylvia and I had discussed this on the ride up to Westchester. I realized that this cycle of crime and violence wouldn't stop without my cooperation. And even then, at best it would be put on pause. My girls were going to be impacted as long as there was a Montenegro involved."

"So you sacrificed yourself?" Eddy offered

Maria let the question hang in the air for a minute before answering.

"Yes. Sylvia didn't like it at all, but I eventually persuaded her that it was for the best. Like with Jackie, Sylvia negotiated my deal, the difference being that we had agreed together on the terms during the ride to meet Mel. It was an outrageous ask, but we knew that the FBI had it in for my brothers. So, I'd give them the goods. They would help me fake a heart attack with carefully administered drugs and an orchestrated medical response team. Beforehand, I redid my will—in the case of an untimely death—to make Sylvia the executor of my estate. I knew she would carry out my wishes to be cremated and that my remaining minor children would be adopted by her family. This allowed me to exit this life without any questions—they burned someone else's body, of course—and go into witness protection knowing that my daughters would be well taken care of and away from the Doble Doble."

"But why are you in New York? And why Mari Diaz? Wasn't she from the neighborhood?"

Maria again laughed.

"Let me answer the second question first. Yes, you have a good memory. Mari Diaz lived in the basement apartment of our building in the Bronx. She was an overprotective mom, whom I happened to get to know before she departed for Queens. What most people don't know is that she and her husband divorced right after the move, and the daughter, looking to get out from under her mother's thumb, went to live with her father. It tore Mari apart. She died shortly after the divorce. Given our similar physical attributes and age, it was easy to assume her identity."

"Hiding in plain sight," Eddy remarked.

"Yes! As to your second question, this apartment is an FBI safe house. I started in witness protection in the middle-of-nowhere Indiana, but I grew tired of the winters. I asked to be moved to Puerto Rico. I was in Toa Baja for many, many years. I recently moved again, hiding in plain sight. Nobody notices an old woman."

"Leaving your girls must have been a very difficult decision."

"Eddy, I have thought about and wrestled with that decision every day. But I know in my heart of hearts it was the right one. I was unable to protect JC. Jackie and I were so young as parents, and JC paid the price. As a mother, I knew I had to protect my girls, no matter the personal cost, because of how I failed JC. And with Jackie gone, I couldn't just leave. Entiendes?"

"Como no." (Of course.)

"Sylvia and Jhonny—bless their souls—were good parents to my girls and allowed them to get away from the stink of my brothers. I have watched very proudly from afar. Sylvia and I met secretly from time to time. With help from the Feds— another condition of my deal—we very carefully and discreetly choreographed visits in out-of-the-way places. Now Sylvia is gone because they thought she was the CI."

"Yes."

"And you're here because it was my brothers again, no?" Maria asked.

"Well, that's the working theory," Eddy said. "I've been able to pull some pieces together, and I'm trying to make them fit."

"Can I help?"

"Maybe, if you don't mind covering some painful history."

"The pain dulls, but it never goes away. I've spent a lifetime dealing with this ache. Go ahead."

"When your husband died, your brothers came to the wake, and one brother in particular opened Jackie's casket to leave him a gift of sorts. Do you remember this?"

"Si. Tomas put a bottle of that hot sauce inside with Jackie."

Knowing to some degree the answer but being careful not to lead the witness, Eddy asked the next question delicately.

"Why?"

Maria's eyes welled up as she searched for the words to answer.

"When we were kids growing up, Jackie spent a lot of time at my family's apartment. He and my brothers were tight. We were all like this big pack of kids hanging around together. My mom invited him to join us for a lot of arroz con pollo, which Jackie loved. My mom bought that pique de isle like it was going out of style. I swear, between Tomas and Jackie, they drank from those bottles. They were crazy for it. As an adult, Tomas bought it by the case and stored it at his home and the shop for himself and Jackie. So, I guess in his diabolical mind, it was a sentimental gift for my husband."

"Interesting."

"Why do you ask?"

Eddy ignored the question for a second and moved on to another.

"In your last visits with Sylvia, did she mention anything about going back to the old neighborhood?"

"No. In fact, she knew that Tomas and my brothers were going to be released from prison, which scared her a bit, and she wanted to remain out of sight. That's why she moved north and never returned. Out of sight, out of mind!"

"Let me ask you a hypothetical question. If Sylvia received a bottle of that hot sauce from an anonymous source with a note saying, 'like brother, like son,' how do you think she'd react?"

Maria's eyes went wide as she cupped her hand to her open mouth.

"Ay dios! My brother did that?"

"Well, not exactly. I think Tomas sent a bottle to Jamie, Sylvia's son, with that specific anonymous note, hoping that he would tell her—which he did—and she'd—"

"Rush in to protect her child." Maria cut him off, finishing his sentence.

"Yes. I believe Tomas used Jamie to call Sylvia out and lure her back to the neighborhood."

"Sylvia never ran from a fight. I think Sylvia sometimes assumed that having my daughters shielded her from the DDs. She believed they'd never do anything to harm them. That bottle and that note would have disabused her of that notion."

Eddy's eyes conferred his agreement.

"With her kids and my girls, she also probably didn't want to wait for the fight to come to her and risk collateral damage. Naturally, she wanted to run toward it."

"That's what I've come to believe, and what you've told me all but confirms my thinking."

"Can you pin it all back to Tomas? Will he pay for her death?"

"Not in any legal sense," Eddy responded evasively.

Eddy asked to use the bathroom. Maria pointed him down a hall and past a bedroom. As he walked past the bedroom, Eddy noticed some luggage—his and hers—with tags that sat at the foot of a bed. Using an old trick, he stopped in front of the room, appearing to sneeze. He turned his head and had his eyes trained toward the inside of the bedroom, and he read something on the tag that suddenly made a lot of sense. The address of the owner was Delray Beach, Florida.

EDDY, JAMIE, AND SOFIA

Jamie was sitting behind his desk with a cigar smoldering in the ashtray. A tumbler of Lagavulin on ice was in his right hand. It was half empty, and this was his second. Eddy had called and said he'd like to stop by the house. Jamie had been on edge since he spoke to him. He asked Sofia to join him, both to save him from having to repeat the information and to have family nearby to steady him.

Eddy sat on the edge of the couch, opposite Jamie's desk. Jamie handed him two fingers of Lagavulin, neat. In between them was a rectangular coffee table with two leather chairs at the farthest corners. Sofia sat in the one to Jamie's left.

"Gordo," Eddy started, but Sofia interrupted with a chuckle at the revival of her brother's childhood nickname.

"Sorry," she said, covering her mouth with her hand

"Anyway ... Gordo, your sense of what happened to your mom, I think, is dead on."

"I knew it!"

"However, all I've done is string together a thesis, but like I said early on, it's only pieces that I've been able to pull together to create a picture. But not enough to uphold an evidentiary standard. Nothing that could be proven in a court of law, entiendes?"

Sofia stifled her urge to bark out and instead leaned in to ask a question framed as an accusation.

"So whoever killed my Mother is going to get away with it?"

Eddy pretended not to hear her inquiry as he revealed what he learned.

"From what I could gather, your mother ..."

Eddy recounted the story to Jamie and Sofia: how Sylvia had met Mel Rubin of the FBI through the tragedy of JC's and Mel's daughter, Lisa's, death; how she subsequently sought his assistance to ensnare the Montenegro Doble Doble by using her brother Jackie without his knowledge; and how the FBI squeezed Jackie to rat on the Doble Doble, but he was found out and eliminated before it could all go down.

"So, she ended up ratting on Tomas and his brothers," Jamie jumped in.

"No." Eddy hesitated before continuing. "Let me explain. You were right about the package of hot sauce. It was a message from Tomas, who had placed a similar bottle of hot sauce in Jackie's casket. Apparently, he stored cases of it at the yard for him and Jackie. The note was a threat on your life with an insinuation that he was responsible for Jackie's death, which I think your moms always suspected. Tomas banked on you telling your mother, inadvertently delivering the message."

"Oh my God!" Jamie and Sofia said out loud in stereo.

Eddy continued.

"Knowing her part in instigating the FBI investigation, your mom felt that she put herself and, by association, her immediate family in Tomas's crosshairs. Her survival instincts kicked in."

"He called her out, and she ran toward him to divert the damage away from us!" concluded Sofia.

"Yes, that's what I believe. In fact, I think Tomas counted on that reaction. He constructed the snatch and grabs on the crotch rockets to bury the real intent and target of their actions."

"This all seems so ... I don't know ... organized ... contrived," said Jamie in a somewhat doubtful tone.

"Tomas had a lot of time behind bars to think and to plot his revenge. He had always been very deliberate, very calculated. I believe that because he knew that Jackie had been approached by the FBI and he'd eliminated that threat, there was only one other person brave enough to move against him and his brothers."

"My mother!" intoned Jamie

"Si! And Tomas had more fuel for his anger when Timoteo was killed while he was in the pen. Sources tell me he held whoever dropped a dime on him and his brothers responsible for his brother's murder at the hands of the Satanic Saints."

"Because his brothers weren't there to protect him. Shit!" Sofia blurted out.

"Yes, and Tomas was dead set on revenge. So not only did he seek out the FBI source, but he settled the score with the Saints. Willy 'Cat Eyes' recently disappeared never to be heard from again."

"Holy shit! It was a whole operation!" Jamie asserted.

Eddy nodded in agreement.

"And I think your Mom's instincts were dead on. She was in Tomas's crosshairs. Apparently, he built up his own black ops team of cyber detectives, a network of criminal intelligence spies to retrace the FBI's case against him and his brothers to find the source."

"And so he did!" said Jamie.

"No, he didn't," Eddy countered.

"I don't understand," Sofia said, jumping in.

"As best as I could piece together, Tomas's intelligence gathering got him enough pieces to suss out your mom's part in the plot, and he became laser focused on that point. It's what we call confirmation bias."

"A bias that occurs when decision makers seek out evidence that confirms their previously held beliefs while discounting evidence that might support a different conclusion," Sofia recited the definition as though she were reading out of a tome on behavioral science.

"Exactly! But the bias led him away from discovering the FBI's *real* source."

"Eddy, I don't get it. You said my mom instigated the investigation?"

"Gordo, I did, and this is what got her killed. But in reality, she merely opened the door. She was not the true CI. Mari Diaz was."

"The overprotective mom?" said Jamie in disbelief.

"Mari Diaz died shortly after leaving the neighborhood—and her identity was assumed by someone very familiar with the Montenegro Doble Doble, someone who stepped forward and became the real source behind the FBI case."

"Oh my God!" the siblings again stated in unison.

"Yes, and Mari is in witness protection."

"Who is she?"

It took every ounce of strength and fortitude on Eddy's part to withhold that bit of information. He felt like the literal cat that ate the canary. Lives, today and forevermore, depended upon his discretion. Mel Rubin and Maria Cruz told him as much when they invited him into the inner circle. They trusted that while the truth might be liberating to them in the telling, it could all be damning for others outside the circle of trust.

While prepping his remarks for Gordo, Eddy knew they would come to this crossroad. He wrestled with the various options, none of them completely satisfying and all of them with their own dead man's switch—once triggered, lives altered, obliterated. He was always a man of the truth and always believed in justice, holding that the facts would be light that would disinfect the germs of lies and crimes. Eddy's mind grappled with this dilemma both then and now as Gordo's question hung in the air. Eddy realized that truth would not set Gordo and his family free. It would distort their sense of history. The only casualty to continuing the lie was Eddy himself. He didn't want to lie to his friend, but he also didn't want to blow up his life either. Eddy could unburden himself of this secret, or he could swallow it down forevermore. He would be burdened with the truth for the rest of his life. He decided to jump on the proverbial grenade and protect those around from the explosion.

He inhaled air deeply into his chest and audibly out through his nose before answering the question.

"I'm not sure." Eddy lied.

For some reason, at this moment Jamie thought about the many times when he would ask his mother too many questions and she would quip, "You writing a book? Well, leave this chapter out and make it a mystery!"

Maybe this was a mystery, and this particular chapter would remain missing.

"Was Mel Rubin involved? Did mom go to him?" Sofia asked, remembering the newspaper clippings and the funeral card for Lisa.

"Yes, in an official capacity with the FBI," Eddy responded.

"Was Mom *involved* with Mel Rubin? He lives in Delray Beach, after all."

"I cannot confirm or deny that."

And before Sofia could add a clarifying follow-up question, Eddy continued.

"I really don't know. But let me tell you what I think I do know."

Jamie and Sofia both nodded.

"Sylvia was a hero! She had the courage to call out what was ugly even if it meant turning her family upside down. She and Mel Rubin shared scar tissue over very heartbreaking circumstances. She used her experiences as a catalyst for constructive change, knowing that it would get very dark before any light would ever appear."

Eddy was surprised by his own poetic recitation, but he continued.

"She sought out Mel Rubin and the FBI to help her in her crusade, and it cost Jackie his life, yet she continued undeterred. But her knowledge of criminal activity among the Doble Doble was not firsthand, so they needed someone inside—someone who did or could get it for them."

"And that was this person, this Mari?" Again, Sofia was reading ahead.

"Yes, and I've concluded that your mother and Mari became friends and confidantes over the years. Mel Rubin, who I believe your mother admired very much, was the connective tissue for this relationship. I think Sylvia's regular trips to those airports were trysts with Mari, and perhaps Mel, but not romantic in nature. I believe they all shared a difficult history, almost like war veterans who served together under circumstances that no one but themselves could truly understand."

"They were familia!" Jamie declared.

"Si, mi hermano, si!" Eddy agreed with his lifelong friend and brother while knowing the true irony in his conclusion.

ANGEL ROJAS

Angel Rojas had unique and special talents honed from years spent in the concrete jungles of New York, as well as the verdant jungles of Southeast Asia and Central America. His skills were highly specialized and very expensive. He was extremely selective in choosing his engagements because they required equal and exhaustive parts planning and discretion. He was very proud of his completion record. His assignments required detailed surveillance, analysis, and stealth. In order to be effective, his end product had to have impact, while he, as architect, had to go completely unnoticed—a ghost or a shadow. In fact, most of his clients did not know his real name. They referred to him as *el espirtitu*, the Spirit.

Angel had recently received a text on his encrypted phone. It was a message from someone he ran with in the Bronx before heading off to Vietnam where he was trained as an army sniper. Distinguished and decorated for picking off the enemy, Angel found little fanfare and appreciation for his work when he returned stateside. The lone exception had been this old friend from the neighborhood, who encouraged him to use his talents to fight imperialism in Central America.

Angel went off to join FARC in Colombia, where his new comrades embraced his speciality and taught him even more about theirs. Angel became a guerrilla warfare legend, kidnapping for ransom and using demolition tactics. He met soldiers, rebels, narcos, peasants, and CIA operatives. He befriended one and all. Many of these factions hired Angel for his varied skill set, especially those talents whose outcomes were fatal and final. Thus began his accidental and lucrative career as an assassin for hire. His old running mate, who had sent him down this path all those years ago, employed him from time to time. He felt somewhat indebted to him. He'd helped him survive the streets and given him an early education to the bonds of a small brotherhood, the Satanic Saints.

The text provided a phone number. Angel knew it was a potential assignment. The text outlined that the position was in the field of waste disposal and required travel to Central America. Angel left his penthouse in Key Biscayne, took his private elevator to his garage, and got into his BMW M8 to drive to South Beach. The engine growled with hunger and then purred with content as he pushed the metallic blue machine beyond the speed limit within seconds. For a man whose chosen profession required discretion, this sleek land shark on wheels turned a head or two as it glided down the street. He entered a restaurant that he owned via a byzantine corporate structure. He nodded to the maître d' and the bartender and headed to the office in the back. When he entered, his operating partner, a rather attractive redheaded Latina, got up from her chair behind her desk—as though on command—kissed Angel on the cheek, and left the office, closing the door behind her. Angel pulled out a phone taped to the bottom of the desk and called the number from the text. He listened to the details of the job, agreed on a price and arrangements for payment—a slight discount for an old friend now seeking revenge—and hung up to make his travel arrangements.

Using his CIA contacts and a small electronic transfer of funds, Angel was able to get satellite and drone images of a remote jungle location in Costa Rica of a new monied residence. It was a compound not far from a small beach town. Its safety features and personnel gave the inhabitant a false sense of security and privacy. Angel knew that no one was untouchable. He estimated it would take a few weeks to study the habits of his target and another few weeks to plot his approach. The planning required the most devotion of time, but the greatest risk came in delivering on the choreography of entry and exit without a trace.

Angel knew this was a revenge hit. He always tried to link the method of elimination to his perceived rationale for the contract. Someone who pursued a scorched-earth policy in life would be consumed in an accidental pyre. Another who looted his former employer would be weighted down with stones and pieces of gold and plunged into the ocean. A double cross earned the perpetrator a double tap to the head.

Weeks later while lounging on the wraparound deck of his Key Biscayne residence with expansive views of the Atlantic, Angel read the *New York Times* online. It was reported that Tomas Montenegro, reputed head of the notorious Doble Doble, recently released from prison had perished suddenly in Costa Rica. Upon leaving his estate in Guanacaste, Costa Rica, Mr. Montenegro's Range Rover exploded with such force that there was little remaining of either the vehicle or Mr. Montenegro. They both, quite literally, disappeared.

Angel took another sip of his coffee and smiled at the precise justice of his work. As instructed by the contract, he texted a prearranged message to another burner phone and then tossed it in the bay.

The message read: "Sangre por Sangre."

EPILOGUE

Sylvia Quintana, wife of the late Jhonny Quintana and mother of Jamie, Sofia, and Charlton, as well as Elena, Milagros, and Celia—the adopted daughters whom she treated as her own, of her predeceased brother Jackie and his wife—died tragically during the commission of a crime. Sylvia is remembered as a loving and nurturing mother, aunt, and loyal friend. A survivor from Spanish Harlem and the South Bronx, she graduated from Morris High School in the Bronx and went to work on Wall Street at Bankers Trust Company, where she managed the legal department. Sylvia was a gracious volunteer for the Catholic Church and Montefiore Hospital. Her children attended Nobles and Greenough, Beaver Country Day, and Choate before graduating from Carnegie Mellon, Bowdoin, Georgetown, and Boston College. In her later years, she was an artist. She will be remembered as a caring person who embodied the American dream. Services at Ortiz's Funeral Home.

A studio-quality picture capturing a smiling Sylvia accompanied the obituary.